The Gooseboy

The Gooseboy

A. L. BARKER

A NOVEL

HUTCHINSON

LONDON MELBOURNE AUCKLAND JOHANNESBURG

This edition first published in 1987 by Hutchinson,
an imprint of Century Hutchinson Ltd,
Brookmount House, 62–65 Chandos Place,
London WC2N 4NW

Century Hutchinson Australia Pty Ltd
PO Box 496, 16–22 Church Street, Hawthorn, Victoria 3122,
Australia

Century Hutchinson New Zealand Limited
PO Box 40–086, Glenfield, Auckland 10, New Zealand

Century Hutchinson South Africa (Pty) Ltd
PO Box 337, Berglvei, 2012 South Africa

British Library Cataloguing in Publication Data

Barker, A.L. (Audrey Lilian)
   The gooseboy.
   I. Title
   823′.914 [F]   PR6052.A647

   ISBN 0-09-172569-0

Printed and bound in Great Britain by
Anchor Brendon Ltd., Tiptree, Essex.

1

Bysshe could be seen, not so old nor so young, walking in his garden, a dusty lusty place of greed and rapine. The fig assaulted the cypress, the bamboo contended with the agave, mats of Bermuda grass smothered the flagstones and the Jerusalem thorn forced up tiles said to be Roman. It was a wilderness which he would one day have to hack his way through, breaching his own solitude. The plants would be at each other's throats as soon as he had passed.

Someone, it turned out, was watching him. He had supposed himself visible only to his private audience, that reliable claque located between his inner ear and eye. Nothing had warned him that he was under observation; the extra senses which he had acquired in his profession were not functioning. The standard five made him supremely conscious of himself, a supremacy which in his youth he had taken as his due, the fact of living. Nowadays he was aware of the brevity of prime and mindful that his might be already past.

This morning, snuffing up every sight and sound, he tasted the green stink of ivy and spread himself in the sun like the basking lizards. He was glad that he could still experience simple appetites and impure joys, it was an assurance that he was human and had not been pushed by circumstance into the upper echelons. But as a public performer he was obliged in his private and even prurient moments to keep up an appearance and would have preferred not to appear as he must have done before this audience of one.

The man had got in the day after his agent had telephoned. Carver came through at 11 p.m., as the day in the Midi was folding. Where Carver was it was early evening; Carver never related to other people's convenience.

'Rexie?'

'Ici le préposé.'

'Rexie, where are you?'

'Ne quittez pas, s'il vous plaît.'

'Get me Eel Murry.'

'Attendez un peu.'

'I want to talk to Lord Snowdon.'

'Quoi?'

'This is the United States of America calling the subcontinent of Europe.'

'J'ai bien compris l'origine de votre appel, monsieur. Patientez un petit peu, nous devons contacter L'Ile Marie.'

Carver had discovered Bysshe playing whodunnits in Bournemouth. He came backstage where Bysshe was trying to unblock the ladies' toilet, having just been carried off as the first murder victim and prior to his next walk-on as a vicar. 'Are you taking this up as a career?'

Carver wore an actual bootlace as a tie. 'Ever thought of going into pictures? What's your name, kid?' he asked.

'Douglas Bysshe.'

'Like in fish?'

'No, it's spelt with two esses and a y, as in Shelley.'

Carver, who was crude, said, 'I don't care if it's spelt with two tits as in Nelly, I don't see Bacall teaming with a name like that. We'll call you Rex, it's dignified and manly. And – I've got it – Snowdon. Rex Snowdon. So people think you're related.'

'Qui est ce Milord, monsieur?'

'You've got Alps over there, haven't you? You've seen the white stuff on top – that's him. Snowdon, the earl of.'

'Don't call me that.'

'Rexie, that you? They talk Chinook where you are. When are you coming back?'

'I'm on holiday.' He might have said 'recovering', but Carver would have jumped to the wrong conclusion.

'You've been away too long. Blood and traffic aren't the only things that circulate. People say to me "*Rex* Snowdon? His name's Tony." I couldn't get you a dandruff commercial.'

He was not here to recoup or reinstate, but to thicken his hide, and there were ways of doing it which he did not understand. It was something to do with the sun. It was all to do with the sun. But not just that: here, of all the places he knew, were assembled the factors for his rearmament.

'Erckmann's going to do a biopic about Zwemmer.'

'Who?'

'Anatole Zwemmer, the leper doctor. They want you.'

'They *want* me?'

'Get the next plane back.'

'Why?'

'Are you asking me? What are you asking me? Can you afford to pass up the chance of a lifetime? Who gets a lifetime? I've talked my ass off and I'm still talking but I can't do it all.'

'You said they wanted me.'

'You're not in the picture yet. You've got competition. Brando for one. He's too old for the young Zwemmer but Erckmann's getting Clint Rose for that. Lancaster's spoken of. Erckmann says it's a deep part. I told him you're the one who can get to the bottom of it. Christ, what's that?'

'Thunder. It's been threatening all day. I can see lightning. We get every kind here, tiny and twitchy like nerve ends, sheet, forked, zigzag, ball –'

'Whassat?'

'We're in for a storm.'

'I didn't call to talk about weather. Why are you hiding? Are you doing a Garbo? Think you've reached the top? Let me tell you, there's a hill of dirt for you to climb yet.'

'Could I do Zwemmer?'

'How do I know? I tell them what's good about you; you're not just a pretty face. You use everything you've

3

got. I tell them if they pick someone who can only lead with his jaw they won't see him act for hair because Zwemmer never shaved. He was homely. Does that bother you?'

'He was a latter-day saint.'

'They're taking the story from his dissolute childhood.'

'Dissolute?'

'He was on the streets by the time he was six.'

'Aren't *I* too old?'

'I don't get you, I don't get anything. This could do for you what *Calcutta* did for Kingsley.'

'*Gandhi.*'

'Gandhi was only in newsreels.'

'I just don't know if I can do Zwemmer.'

'My Gud –' Bysshe had often wondered if Carver benefited by having a personal deity – 'for years you complained about being typecast, said you were sick of romantic roles. At your age your worries on that score are over. But here's a second chance. They're taking the film on location and it'll be one hundred per cent real – cultural elevation with guts. Zwemmer was a fashionable surgeon in his day, he made more with his knife than Ford with his motors.'

Rex/Douglas – which did he dislike most? Snowdon, without doubt. The press had fun with it and the daughters of America claimed to see a likeness. One woman had asked was it on his father's or his mother's side, whereupon her friend had shrieked with shame that everyone knew the mother's name was Armstrong-Jones. 'Bysshe' was rightfully his, and there were the other matters of 'Music, when soft voices die', 'My name is Ozymandias, king of kings: Look on my works, ye Mighty, and despair!'

He wanted the part: he who had been the object, or more truthfully the objective, of the simulated passion of nymphets, mouth to mouth – more murder than resuscitation – and the pressure of countless scene-stealing busts on his rib-cage. He wanted to do Zwemmer, of whom he knew only that he had gone to Africa and lived among lepers at a time when the civilized, and uncivilized, world banished them to hives in the jungle.

'What happened to him?'

'He went to the river and didn't come back. The crocs ate him.'

'He could still be alive.'

'He'd be one hundred and thirty-five years old. The final scene will be unfocused fade-out, the sun coming through the jungle, lighting up his halo or was it his hat. Quality movie.'

'Did they actually ask for me?'

'Why would they ask for you? They think you've only done skinflicks. It was me said you could act. I made myself believe it.'

'Thanks.'

'You've got the chance and that's all you've got. Erckmann's toying with the idea of Charlie Palk.'

'Palk does Westerns.'

'Did that stop Cooper? Or Grant? Or Newman? If Larry Oliver could do a dance routine and *King Lear*, why should you fret?'

'I'll call you tomorrow.'

'Call from the airport or don't bother.'

Tomorrow and tomorrow and tomorrow, but what Bysshe by-rights meant was the hypothetical time when he might be ready. And who would wait for that? Not Carver, not the world, not anyone. Erckmann wouldn't even look round.

After Carver hung up, he heard the frogs. Carver's voice had drowned theirs. Carver's voice, over the wire, was the essence of the man as distinct from his assemblage. One could do equally well without his factors: it wasn't necessary to see his blue mountainous face and smell fifty glorious years of Bourbon on his breath to be caught up in his indecent haste. Carver seemed to be tearing through life to get to the best bit. Tomorrow and tomorrow: Bysshe was waiting, and Carver running, and they would both end up with only their yesterdays. Like everyone else.

The frogs by night, the cigalles by day, and the clicking, ticking, rustling, bustling of his anarchic

5

garden was what sustained Bysshe; the knowledge that the garden was in the recycling business and that hell and high water, when they came, would only accelerate the cycle. Carver would have said, 'Tape the frogs and bugs if they mean so much and bring the tape to LA and play it for vibes.' What Carver didn't know was that in his contemplative moments Bysshe would lie with his face to the ground, appreciating every skeletal leaf and cannibal ant and willing the detritus to crumble or pupate or jell or in some way evolve before his eyes. He had resigned himself to wait and was hoping to use this summer to acquire a scarfskin.

He slept badly that night. Thinking of Zwemmer and knowing so little about him, Zwemmer got grafted on to Carver and appeared in his dreams as a blue-bearded hustler in a pith helmet, sweating whisky and jeering at Rex Snowdon for being unable to portray an odour of sanctity.

Soon after dawn he rolled off his bed and went naked into the garden, thrusting his feet through the St Barnaby thistles. He felt the need of a positive spite after the cloudy malice of the dream. He cracked his ankle on the roots of an olive. The wood was cool; it first chilled, then burned him to the bone.

The grains of darkness were running out of the sky, and from the point where it was possible to see the sea – though not to desire it, for the shores were polluted and degraded – the light magnified his nerve endings. He took refuge under the dark leaves of a carob tree in this, his favourite hour, when he was sure of being alone.

The garden itself was walled. Under the walls were ditches, into the top of the walls were cemented fragments of wine bottles; real glass, green and yellow and barbarous. The padlocked gate was knitted up with barbed wire. The house itself was hidden from the road by olives and gorse and tamarisk. There would appear little incentive to break through to it.

Years ago it would have been a lustrous folly, all-white, with balconies, fretted shutters, curly eaves and domed roof: a Taj Mahal from the chines of

Bournemouth. It was chalky now, and cracked like a clown's face. The woodwork was gently discharging itself: Bysshe had been greatly heartened when he first witnessed the operation, slivers drifting to the ground as they might be moths or stale snowflakes, being seized and carried off by ants. Not a grain, not a particle ignored. It cheered him to know that his house was contributing to the recycling business.

But there had been interlopers, despite the decay. Walls, padlocks and the general air of grot didn't deter the most persistent. The Rex Snowdon fan club in Danceville/Deever/Tarkoe or somewhere, arrived and battered at his gate. When admittance was denied them, the maturer members tried to climb over. Two had spiked themselves on the wire: another, even more mature, fell and fractured her coccyx. Rex Snowdon was obliged to come out of hiding and organize first aid, whereupon the uninjured mobbed him. Heedless of their wounded, they reached for him with the lust of predators.

Once he had found a girl under his bed. She refused to come out. She had seen him in *The Consul's Lady* eight times in Pittsburgh and five in Tusa and in other places, she said. She was a travelling beautician and moved around. It was dusty under his bed and she had scrambled through the gorse and over the wire and a beautician need not be beautiful any more than a doctor need be healthy. Kneeling, with her elbows on the floor, she had glared at Bysshe from between the bedsprings. She was wearing giant horn-rimmed spectacles and reminded him of the dog with eyes like saucers in the fairy tale.

Sighing, he had locked the door on her and passed the night in one of the guest rooms. The girl in possession of his bed and the irrelevance of her being there only seemed like one of a string of irrelevancies which had started in his pram.

In the morning, inspired by an uncharitable notion, he had taken the oieboy upstairs. The girl was resting peacefully on his bed. He pushed the boy into the room and awakened her by kicking the leg of the bed.

Opening her eyes, she got the full shock view of the boy's face – the wrong or, in this case, the right side. One look was enough. She screamed, sprang off the bed and ran as if a devil of hell was after her.

Bysshe thought of privacy as a prisoner thinks of freedom, as the state of being, and all else mere existence. Achieve privacy and be assured. As an actor, it was virtually impossible for him to be sure of anything. Carver had threatened to make him the World's Lover. 'Why not? Pickford was the World's Sweetheart. Times change, people don't. They want someone to sweep them off their feet. Look at history: Joan of Arc and Joe Louis, Adolf Hitler – he was German and he didn't happen here, but the Kennedys did. It could be you next, Rexie. The lover with the fully comprehensive range.'

Bysshe might hazard a guess, but Rexie knew what was meant by that. Rexie had done some blue-black films to make ends meet, and the memory of them enlivened his nightmares. Repugnance was legitimate but he feared that in making those films he had utilized feelings which were genuinely his own.

The watcher was in the strawberry patch, eating strawberries and making no attempt to hide. He squatted, groping the plants, pulling off the fruit and watching Bysshe. Well he might. Bysshe had been enjoying himself. A sense of absolute uniqueness had set him leaping, singing and clapping out a rhythm on his buttocks in the purity and privacy of his morning garden. Like Adam before Eve.

He saw the man and stopped in mid-caper. The song died in his throat, he teetered on one leg. In his rush of anger he could have killed the fellow, but wiping him out would not wipe out the vision he had of himself. It had passed from the man's eye to his, a camera-shot which he wouldn't be able to forget. He lowered his leg, let his hands drop to his sides and stood naked, trying to look unashamed.

'Surprise, eh?' prompted the man.

'What the hell are you doing here?'

'Surprise all round – as the dog said to the lamp post.'

'This is private property.'

'No kidding.' The man laughed with a forced conviviality which Bysshe found infuriating.

'I can charge you with breaking and entering.'

'I haven't broken anything. I used an old commando trick; I'm pleased I can still do it.'

'Then get out the same way you got in.'

'I can't. There aren't any ditches this side and the way it's done –'

'I don't give a sod how it's done.'

'You never used to cuss.'

'Just get out.'

'Dulcie didn't approve of cussing. Whenever I catch myself doing it, I say that's a sin according to Dulcie. But it doesn't stop me. Some of us are born to blaspheme. I used to say to her, "I could do worse", and she used to say, "What could be worse than offering a direct insult to the Almighty?"'

'I don't know what you're talking about.'

'I mean to say, if sin's original –' Bysshe did not miss the direction of the man's grin, pink-stained teeth chumbling strawberry pulp – 'we can't be held accountable. Dulcie maintained it was our duty to better ourselves.' Bysshe covered his privates with his hand, a reflex activated by mention of the name more than any impulse of modesty. 'She was a god-fearing girl. I'd go further and say she was an angel.'

'You can go to hell.'

The man rose up from the strawberry bed. 'You don't remember me.'

'No.'

'Tom Ewing.' He came across, sticking out his hand as if they were meeting at a party.

Bysshe turned his back and went into the house. In an hour, or less, there would be scarcely a cool place in the garden, but he had been standing in a bar of shadow and was shivering. He put on a bathrobe.

The man calling himself Tom Ewing came up the steps to what Gluvas, the gardener, called the 'terrasse'. The paving stones had tipped, each to a different depth, a different angle, like a scattered pack of cards. They looked as if a touch would straighten them. Ewing appeared to consider it. He toed a slab, then stooped and seized it with both hands. His shoulders could be seen bunching with effort, his knees stood up atavistically beside his ears. He was not a man who would care how he looked and he was right not to. Bysshe classified people by their looks, but realized that those without any had the ultimate advantage over him because they had nothing to lose.

He stood beside Ewing, noting and half envying his bald patch and the comedores on his nose. 'Leave it.'

Ewing tried to prise up the slab. His neck turned puce with tension. 'It wants re-settling. I had the same trouble with my patio at home.'

The word 'patio' identified him, and thus was he rendered harmless. Bysshe had a vision of the same rump suspended to the sound of mowing machines and the smell of Sunday roasts. 'I don't know you from Adam.'

A retort could be made to that, with the laugh on him, but Ewing was too disappointed at not shifting the stone to take the opportunity. 'Can't you get someone to do it for you?'

'I don't want it done. I prefer it as it is, I prefer everything as it is. Saving your presence, which I can do without.'

'They told me you don't encourage visitors. I was in the fish market and they slit up a fish to show me the sort of welcome I could expect.'

'The fish market?'

'In the town. The cabbie who brought me said it was a publicity gimmick.'

'I don't give interviews or charity chats or autographs, and I'm giving you one minute to get out.'

'If you don't remember me, what about this?' Ewing pulled something out of his pocket and thrust it at Bysshe.

It was the figure of an animal of some sort, crudely stamped out of metal and painted municipal green. As Bysshe turned it over, his memory unwillingly, resentfully, stirred.

'Tearing through the countryside, up and down the

roads, in and out of people's gardens, round and round the war memorial. We were tearaways,' Ewing said proudly, 'and we each had one of these on the handlebars of our bikes. We called ourselves the Green Dragons.'

It was not a time Bysshe wanted to recapture. Pubescence had been a pain. He had ridden his old Ariel in rages of frustration and disgust, and a form of joy which he had believed to be special until he understood that it was surrogate sex. And he had suffered with acne. The thing in his hand was chipped and shabby, barely recognizable as a rampant beast. All it did now was evoke a shabby time.

'Those were the days,' said Ewing, 'free as birds and larger than life.'

'We were a bunch of skinny kids on clapped-out motorbikes.'

'Mine was new. I forged my father's signature as guarantor and got it on the never-never.'

'I don't remember you.'

'After I crashed it and lost my licence I rode pillion. I rode to Glasgow with you to your cousin's wedding.'

'My cousin lived in Edinburgh.'

'Where I first saw your sister.'

'Which sister?'

'You only had one.'

Bysshe tossed him the metal dragon. 'I'm going to make coffee.'

'*You* were skinny. Who'd have thought you'd be a film star.'

'Why have you come?'

'To see you.' That was what they came for, the travelling beautician, the Danceville crowd, the snoopers on the hill with picnics and telephoto lenses. Out of some sort of priapic curiosity. Ewing grinned mateily. 'I've seen all of you.'

'How did you know where I live?'

'The cabbie knew.' Ewing followed him into the house. 'You never were friendly. We called you "Jeeper's Creeper".'

'Did you?' Bysshe was pleased. So he might indeed be

11

the right one to play Zwemmer, the private man forced into a public situation.

'You're comfortable.' Ewing was looking round the kitchen.

Dishes waited to be washed. A cat slept in a basket with peaches. The windowsill was crowded with petrified cactus plants. 'I expected something a bit different.'

'I came here to forget things like emptying the teapot.'

'And putting on your clothes.'

'I remember to take them off.'

'You married?'

'No.'

Ewing made a grimace of pure misery. 'I am. An air hostess. She brought me down to earth.'

Bysshe turned from putting on the coffee to scrutinize his visitor. Ewing wouldn't be able to lose or control the solid fat which was accumulating over his hips, not converting its sugar, not doing its chemistry, putting him at risk. His shoulders were hooped with the premonition of it.

It struck Bysshe as significant that a gangling youth – although he could not recall Ewing in any detail, they had all been gangling – should carry within him the shape and substance of his self to come, like a woman with child. But a man was committed, without the hope of an abortion, to producing himself.

There were times, looking in his mirror, when he saw what he himself was bringing forth: a man who could be credited with integrity and a lot of living. His features were still well-defined, his waist and hips still localized, his hair still plentiful with as yet only a few white cottons in it. Only his eyes singled him out from other well-structured men, possessing as they did a deep and irrevocable hurt. It was always there, he had checked on it at mundane moments. While he was shaving or tying his tie or licking a postage stamp his eyes looked hurt, though it was a poignant awareness that he could locate nowhere else in himself. 'If you didn't have eyes like an organ-grinder's monkey you'd still be playing stiffs in Bournemouth,' Carver had told him. But his face was changing, sharpening, awakening. Hawks' eyes were cold, inimical, and the valuable hurt would soon be lost.

'If I had your chances,' said Ewing, 'I know what I'd do. It's not your looks or your success I envy, it's your freedom.'

Bysshe's snort woke the cat. Freedom – when it was a question now of what he could do, what he was capable of, and would be allowed to try. Carver was right. Nobody was going to look for his potential any more, he would have to put himself over. And his potential could be nullified by commercial considerations. 'Show business is the biggest bondage there is.'

'I wouldn't mind being bonded.'

'Do you like your coffee black?'

'Who's that?'

The oieboy had come into the yard, his arms full of brown roses. He carried them carefully, his head bowed, solicitous, even tender. The dead petals were falling in showers and he kept stopping to lift each foot and shake it, like a cat on hot bricks in slow motion.

'He lives here.'

'He's pretty.'

'It depends how you look at him.'

'How *I* look at him?' Ewing was a bad winker, had trouble uncoordinating his eyes.

Bysshe went to the window and whistled. The boy put up his face to the sky. Bysshe whistled again, a short blast such as he might use to alert an accomplice or summon an animal. The boy threw down the roses and came to the window. His jeans were soiled and too big for him, so that his body could be seen moving with grace inside the bloated cotton. For grace of movement he could be relied upon, and the sun, doing its bit, shot to blazes every wire-gold hair on his head.

Ewing said, 'Are you going to introduce me?'

The boy was a few feet away, his head turned to one side. He tended to look sideways, probably because he could see more clearly with one eye than with the other. Bysshe pointed along the terrasse. The boy followed the direction of his finger and the sun which had irradiated his hair did the same to the left side of his face.

Ewing gasped. 'Christ almighty!'

Bysshe smiled the smile which complemented the hurt in his eyes and had persuaded so many women that he was looking only to them for comfort. 'I fancy the damage is secular.'

'What?'

Bysshe whistled again and made a dismissive gesture. The boy, turning to look, presented the perfect right side of his face, with a scarlet geranium looped over one ear.

'How did he get like that?'

'Nobody knows.'

'Bloody hell,' said Ewing. 'It gave me a turn.'

'The first time's the worst.' Considerately, Bysshe poured him a tot of marc.

'It's obscene. How can you stand having him around?'

'I don't see him often. He keeps to the orchard and the hillside. He sleeps in the gardener's shed and looks after the geese.'

'Geese?'

'Toulouse geese. They're excellent watchdogs and they live off the land. He's probably taken them to the orchard, otherwise they'd have raised the alarm when you came.' After the Danceville invasion Bysshe had introduced the geese, reasoning that they were more alarmist than dogs, cheaper, and less corruptible. And natural enemies of women.

'So if they don't keep people out, his Sunday face will.' Ewing drained his brandy. 'Suppose I'd had a dicky heart.'

'Then you wouldn't have been jumping over my wall.'

'What does he say? About the way he looks?'

'He doesn't say anything about anything. I've never heard him speak.'

'You mean he's dumb?'

'And deaf to all but high-pitched sounds.'

'Poor little bastard. Where did he come from?'

'Over the wall. Like you.'

One day Bysshe had gone to the slopes of La Roquette and found the boy escorting the geese with a forked stick.

14

They appeared to have no objection, though Bysshe had. While they waited amicably, he questioned the boy. Getting no response he had tried to hustle him off. The birds at once advanced, clanging, their round inimical eyes fixed on Bysshe, and snapped at his legs. 'The geese can take care of themselves. He gets his food and a shakedown and something for helping Gluvas about the place. He's settled here.'

Ewing sighed. 'I stick my neck out, I tend to nowadays. My wife says I'm getting stupid. She comes from a different world.'

'You mean she's extraterrestrial?'

'What I mean,' said Ewing, without dignity, 'is we're not in the same class. My father was a potato merchant and hers managed a shoe shop. I went to the comprehensive, she went to a secondary modern. She makes it matter.'

'You married a high flier.' Bysshe did not stifle his yawn. 'Did you bring her with you?'

Ewing shook his head, peered uneasily through the window. 'Has the kid gone?'

'He'll be in the orchard.'

'What I mean to say, if I'd been to grammar school and my old man worked in an office, she'd take me for what I am. Whatever that is.'

His lips pushed out like a hurt child's. Bysshe, who was wondering how soon he could be rid of him, asked where he was staying.

'I haven't booked in. I got off the train and came straight here.'

'I'm flying to New York today.' Bysshe was surprised and not displeased to hear himself say it. The matter seemed to have been resolved and his objections blown wide open. They were prompted merely by natural disinclination and contrary to his interests.

The whole man should refuse nothing, his duty was to experience. 'I expect to start on a major new film.' Ewing sat staring as if he had all the time in the world and didn't want it. 'I shall be leaving almost at once.'

'What happened to Dulcie?'

'What should happen to Dulcie?'

15

'Is she married?'

'The last time I heard, she was.'

The last time was when Dulcie Pike, née Bysshe, had explained to him the condition of wedlock. He ran into her on the occasion of a family funeral. Ran into, when his intention had been to run out. He had taken a wrong turning among the graves and come face to face with his sister as she picked her way reverently past the floral tributes. 'Bingo!' she had cried, and snatched at him – she probably did indulge in that deadly game – 'you're not going to sneak away, I want to talk to you.' Talk she did, about her husband, whom she referred to in Dickensian style only as 'Pike'.

Bysshe believed that the fact that he and she had shared their mother's womb was the origin of the contention between them. It was in the womb that she had acquired her resentment. To Bysshe, with full partiality and no justice, had been given the favour of the gods. It had been a matter of common consent, people looked into their double pram and said how funny it was – 'funny' was the word their mother, a guileless woman, used – that the prettiest of the twins wasn't the girl.

'What's he like, Dulcie's husband?'

'Not a man I want to remember.'

'She was pure in heart.' Something had got into Ewing, or it had been there all the time and was finally getting out. 'I knew as soon as I saw her.'

'How soon was that?'

'At your cousin's wedding. In Glasgow.'

'Edinburgh.'

'She sang "Love's Old Sweet Song". I'll never forget it.'

Nor would Bysshe. Dulcie he remembered as a source of embarrassment: she had too much femininity. Her disposition, and her figure, had been aggressively female since she had risen five. There was nothing she could have done about it, but she kept on with little-girl and kitten play until her developed and developing bust was forcing up the hem of her gymslip. Bysshe often had to look away. It used to worry him to think that his flesh

16

was the same mix as hers, and he was afraid of it getting the better of him, as it had of her. Then, when she was thirteen and Bysshe still struggling with acne and hot flushes, she suddenly became a woman, missing puberty altogether. Dulcie became in some contentious but undeniable way, mature. She had enjoyed watching his emergent manhood emerging in the wrong places, she who might then have looked away. It was a happy time for her; even her voice, which had been a whine, strengthened to a rich contralto.

'It was a revelation,' said Ewing.

'I thought so.' Bysshe had seen the women dabbing their eyes and the men looking into their beer and the newlyweds locked in a death-defying kiss. 'I wonder if what was revealed to you was the same as was revealed to me.'

'I was a roughneck, a yob. Dulcie made me realize there's more to life than taking what you want.'

'Indeed?'

'What I mean to say, I was out for all I could get, I didn't know how to give.'

'And my sister showed you?'

Darker blood coloured Ewing's jaw. 'She wasn't that sort.'

'Indeed,' Bysshe said again, without question.

'I didn't know I had anything to give. She made me realize I had to give myself.' Ewing, who had given to his air hostess, stared at Bysshe with dismay.

'Oughtn't you to have married Dulcie?'

'I wasn't good enough, quality-wise. But you see, with her it was *me* that was under par, not where I came from.' Ewing, whom Bysshe would have supposed an immodest man, seemed to think he had made an essential point. 'I've always remembered her, she's always at the back of my mind, if not right in front. I mean to say, a girl like her was special.' The confession excited Ewing, he leaned over and punched Bysshe lightly on the shoulder. 'When they open me up they'll find "Dulcie" stamped through me like Brighton through a stick of rock.'

Credulity was not one of Bysshe's failings. In his

17

profession he was obliged to turn everything inside out and examine it. He did so now, and concluded that Ewing had come, not to eulogize Dulcie but to extort money. It would have to be a lot of money to make the trip worthwhile.

'Tell me where she is. I don't even know if she's –' Ewing licked his lips without pleasure – 'alive. I mean to say.'

'Oh, she's around.'

'The day before yesterday it was, I was getting the car out and I pressed the starter like I've done a million times and I thought it's no good, I've got to know. You'd think I'd been working up to it, but I swear to God I hadn't. Not knowingly. It just came over me. I dropped everything and I'm here because you're the only one who can tell me.'

Bysshe, doing a thorough job, turning out the seams, thought that Ewing could be cherishing some idea of blackmailing him. About what? For whose protection? Dulcie's?

'Don't get me wrong. Keeping her in my thoughts has been enough. Till now. The day before yesterday my wife said something, and after that it wasn't enough.'

'What did she say?'

'She said I had no background.'

The unknown quantity of Ewing's wife, all unknown to Bysshe and probably not much known to Ewing, dwindled between them. Dulcie remained, a sacred relic, if you please. Ewing, dewy-eyed, was obviously pleasing, and it was no occasion for pity. His delusion might serve him better than his common sense, as delusions often did.

'You don't mean to say –' it was catching but things could be too simple – 'you came here looking for a background?'

'Twenty years ago I fell for your sister. The moment I saw her I knew what she was.'

'What was she?'

'A pure woman, and I'm proud I had the wit to see it. Sometimes I think it says more for me than anything else I've done.'

18

'You could be right. Did the taxi driver have a ponytail?'

'What?'

'The one I'm thinking of wears his hair long and tied back with an elastic band. He charges double to bring people here; he tells them they'll be asked in to see the live show.'

'I don't know what he charged, I gave him a note and he kept it.'

'We aren't identical twins, Dulcie and me. Not from the same egg.' He had had to fight for his life from the beginning and the idea was repugnant: two specks jockeying for position in the amniotic fluid. 'We're as different as chalk and cheese.'

'Chalk and gold.'

Bysshe felt the wry satisfaction which a flagrant miscasting always afforded him. 'We were never close.' As a child he had been crowded out. Her presence filled the house, filled everywhere. So did her absence. As a child he went in mortal awareness of her, she blew him apart like a dandelion clock. Only in clandestine moments was he able to get himself together and be what he was entitled and intended to be. 'Being twins, they tried to make us a pigeon pair. They had us photographed sitting side by side, but my grandmother cut Dulcie out of the picture and had me enlarged and put in a silver frame.'

'Why?'

Bysshe shrugged. 'People judge by appearances, Dulcie's qualities weren't immediately apparent.' They had never resolved the problem of twinship. It had been a problem, despite their separate eggs; God knew what a kerfuffle it would have been had they split one egg between them. The battle had been for life, and every particular of it. Having appropriated the female gender as the most likely to succeed, Dulcie had coveted the best of the male attributes as well, and had overcompensated with feminine ones. Overdoing it had become a habit. Bobbishness was the armour wherein she trusted. She bobbed everywhere, up and down, in and out, and bobbing, could not be held accountable.

19

'Where is she?' Ewing was looking at Bysshe as if Bysshe were a packet which contained something he badly wanted.

Bysshe, when bored, was wont to provide himself with a scenario. He decided to encourage Ewing. It would be doing him a kindness and Dulcie something less than harm. He sighed. 'I don't suppose I shall see her again.'

'Why not?'

'It's a long story.'

'I want to hear it.'

'I haven't time, I've got to pack.'

'I'm not going till you tell me.'

Bysshe, hastily assembling a few facts, hoped that others would present themselves in the telling. 'You could come with me on the plane and I'd fill you in on the way to New York.'

'You're not going anywhere.' Ewing stood up, stood in the doorway, legs apart, arms folded. It was wonderfully hopeless, the wonder evidenced by how a man could carry a straw in the belief that it was carrying him. Saints and martyrs did, but had there ever been a straw like Dulcie?

'I don't know that I ought to tell you. She wouldn't care to have her private life discussed with a stranger.'

'I'm not a stranger.'

Dulcie of course would have preferred to do the talking: she was about as private as a highway hoarding. 'Sit down, you're making me jumpy.'

Ewing was without grace, and suspicious. He hooked a chair with his foot, positioned it between Bysshe and the door, sat astride and ordered, 'Get on with it.'

Dulcie had come once to Ile-Marie, just after Bysshe had acquired the place. Nothing had been done, the shutter bolts were rusted solid and no window could be opened, there was a pool on the floor of the kitchen with some curious creatures knotted on the bottom, and the salle-à-manger smelt of what he suspected was pot.

He was camping out in the garden at the time and had feared that she would spoil everything and he would have to leave. Then he realized that the place was on his side. No power on earth, she said, and meant it, would

20

get her here again. She was sorry she had come. She had wanted to see how her famous brother lived; and now she could go back to Sidcup and tell them he lived in a stinking ruin.

'Does the name Genghis Pike mean anything to you?'

'What?'

'It's not a name you'd soon forget –' Bysshe loved the 'Genghis' – 'it was front-page news in the *Nursing Mirror*.'

'What are you talking about?'

'The man Dulcie married. Pike by name, Pike by nature. I don't know what she saw in him.' (What Pike had seen in her was womanhood, superabundance: it must have seemed limitless.) 'I think she married him on the rebound.' That much was irrefutable, her being a bouncer. 'There was someone she really cared about in a big way, the once-in-a-lifetime way, and it hadn't worked out. I don't know why. Perhaps,' Bysshe gazed steadily and innocently at Ewing, 'he didn't declare himself. Perhaps he didn't realize how she felt about him. She never spoke of it. My guess is that she fought back by taking Pike, although crève cœur is not a sound basis for marriage.'

'What's not?'

'Heartbreak.'

'She would never do anything that wasn't right.'

'All I know is it wasn't right for her to marry Pike. He was in pharmaceuticals, ran a small business making vapour rub and fruit salts. The firm's trademark was a picture of the founder with walrus moustache and choke collar. That sort of thing inspires confidence. A lot of people swear by the old remedies. Have you heard of Pike's Patent Painkiller?' Ewing shook his head. 'Well, it was a respectable family firm and they did nicely. Then they brought out a new product. It was supposed to be a blood purifier. They called it Pike's Perfecta, and the inference was that whatever you had, or didn't have, would be taken care of. A dose a day to give you germ-free blood, a strong ticker, and the do-it-yourself of a stud bull. Pike himself – I have to say it – was a good advertisement for his medicine. He looked a world-beater. Of course the stuff sold like hot cakes or, I should say, like a panpharmacon.'

'A what?'

'A universal remedy.' Bysshe saw a glint in Ewing's eye which might be suspicion. 'It's funny how people think their blood's to blame for everything. But that medicine made some pretty bad blood. People lost their teeth and their hair. Genghis was raking in the money and he didn't care.'

'Who?'

'Genghis Pike, Dulcie's husband. The BMA stepped in and he was struck off, or whatever they do. He was ordered to pay compensation, but the business finances couldn't sustain it. Genghis was discredited and absconded with what cash and valuables he could lay his hands on.'

'Swine!'

'Oh now,' Bysshe said reasonably, 'he couldn't be blamed for wanting to stay out of jail.'

'Did they catch him?'

'He's not been seen from that day to this.'

'And Dulcie? What happened to Dulcie?'

It was what Ewing wanted to hear, knowledge he had come over land and sea for, powered by some mysterious urge which you could call love – you had to, there was nothing else to call it. Curiosity wasn't enough, passion too much. Love was what Rex Snowdon was known for and could, by means of tried and trusted stimuli which he had learned to administer to himself, enact as promptly as Pavlov's dogs. He could put on a demonstration not to be distinguished from real, whereas Tom Ewing, who knew real, couldn't demonstrate it. He leaned forward, fixing Bysshe with a furious eye. 'What happened to her?'

Ewing as lover, even with lower-case letter, was unlikely, to say the least. And Dulcie as the beloved was sheer pantomime. But it had to be possible that there was more than one love style.

'Genghis Pike and his Perfecta happened. You'd think she'd have had enough. Any other woman would have disassociated herself, gone where she wasn't known, changed her name, made a big mystery and enjoyed it.'

'Enjoyed it?' For Ewing, of course, there wasn't any other woman, there was only Dulcie, his Perfecta. He wouldn't see that there might be too much woman, or that merciful Nature would have made up Dulcie's quota with man and beast if Dulcie hadn't forestalled her. He rose from his chair. 'Where is she?'

'Looking after the sick.'

'Sick?'

'The people who swallowed Pike's medicine. If you were bald and toothless you'd feel sick.' Rage or determination – or was it desire? – had suddenly increased Ewing's girth. He stood, his shirt drum-tight over his chest, his neck as square as a newel-post. Bysshe spoke gently, 'It wouldn't help to know where she is. You couldn't see her, except through a grille.'

'A what?'

'Like they have in prison doors. And travelling cages. A convent is virtually a prison, but it was of her own choosing.'

'You mean she's become a nun?' Ewing's complexion, naturally unrefined, turned meaty.

'Joined a silent order.' For Dulcie that would be fate worse than death. Bysshe did not envisage actual bodily harm for her, only a lifelong martyrdom. And incarceration in a nunnery, especially a speechless one, would ensure that. 'You could talk to her, but she's not allowed to answer.' Dulcie wouldn't thank him for fixing her up with such an image, but he hoped it contented Ewing.

Of course Ewing owed it to himself to demolish the nonsense, but to do so he would have to question Dulcie's sanctity. Bysshe saw the difficulty. What was instructive was the way his own subconscious had evolved the nonsense. It was a cartoon version of the Zwemmer story, the instruction plainly being that he was already committed. He was being worked on. It had to happen with any role but was usually a conscious and

23

unseemly process. The memory of getting himself ready for his scenes in *The Consul's Lady* still revolted his stomach.

'I don't want to talk to her.'

'What *do* you want?'

'Something to go on.'

'Haven't I given you that?' If Ewing asked for more it would be tiresome. 'I've given you background.' The scene should finish with a shot of Ewing's emotively twitching jaw as he turned away. 'Tell your wife that before you met her you were in love with a latter-day saint.'

'When's the next bus to the station?'

'There isn't, and there's no station till Antibes. I'll call you a car and take you to the gate.'

'I can find my own way out.'

'The gate's locked, barred and bolted.'

'What are you afraid of?'

'I'm protecting my seclusion. There have been interlopers less disinterested, or should I say more interested, than you.'

Ewing gave a dry spit of disgust. Bysshe picked up the kitchen extension and phoned Gluvas's grandson who drove an old Maigret saloon. When he put down the receiver Ewing said, 'Were you codding me?'

'Certainly not. Technically the unconsenting male is not as vulnerable as the female, but there are more ways than one of rape.'

'About Dulcie I mean.'

'Why should I?'

Ewing did not know. He would carry the doubt with him, forever unable to resolve it.

'Have you got a bit of paper?'

'What for?'

'For you to write your name on. Rex Snowdon. That's the sort of background my wife likes.'

With Ewing gone, everything started up again. It always did after people had been: business was resumed with joyful frenzy. The business of detrition and metamorphosis. Visitors were an interruption. When

24

Dulcie came there had been a virtual freeze.

Bysshe felt the resumption within himself. His need of privacy and the need of the place coincided. The discipline was transmutation which, after all, was his chosen profession, chosen before he had had time to put two and two together, when he had known in his bones that the answer would come out wrong. He might say that every part he had played, every simulated passion, every embrace, every rubberoid kiss, was a step in the same direction.

He found the idea both comic and comforting. Here he was taken care of, along with the frass and the peace-loving olives. At Ile-Marie he could at last evolve.

The hard shoulder of sky under the carob tree had turned cobalt blue. Mornings were the worst, but not here; here mornings were best, although the nights weren't so good. Sometimes, bedtimes, he needed somebody. Some other body, because that was one thing he didn't do alone. Of course he could supply himself: occasionally he invited someone to stay, or went purposely to Nice or Antibes, but purpose in that connection was aborting. He preferred to take his pleasure randomly, allow himself to be tempted.

The geese were honking on the hillside. They did not discriminate between living and inanimate objects. He had known them be provoked by a burst mattress in a ditch. The gaggle instinct moved them as one, and they stretched their necks, splayed their clowns' feet and gave the alarm. As they had done for the Romans, probably in this same place. In two thousand years they had found nothing better to be than geese.

He couldn't afford to wait a thousand days nor a thousand hours. If he went to New York and played Zwemmer he might break the time barrier and become different overnight: if he went to New York and did not play Zwemmer he could become a turd.

At the back of his mind was the memory of some bloomy old frames of Anatole Zwemmer sitting with a group of his lepers like a captain with his football team. They had no eyes, no hands, and lion faces.

Carver was promising real jungle and real animals

and would have promised real leprosy if he had thought of it. That was the sort of job Make-Up would revel in. Bysshe had watched the transformation of Billy Muir for his part as a thing from the grave. They gave him a rubber skull with tufts of yak hair punched in, the skin of an egg over one eyeball, fully credible maggot holes, and a jaw of plastic teeth like a cowcatcher. A peruke, a tricorn hat and latex cobwebs completed the vision. It wasn't Make-Up's fault, or Billy's, that when he stepped out of his coffin on the set he resembled an Edwardian lady motorist in travelling veil stepping out of her tourer. On screen the effect was chilling enough.

Fake leprosy would whet the public's morbid appetite, Bysshe's job would be to interpret what the real thing might have done to Zwemmer. There was something he had to do before that, something more important and much more difficult. He had to act the man who could act Zwemmer.

Perhaps he should read up on him, obit notices and whatever biographies there were. Except that Erckmann would have discarded all there was to know and would have put together, or be keeping on the boil, a lot of irrelevant facts and fantasies of his own.

Erckmann was known as a spellbinder. Certainly he worked like a charm – entirely without reason. Carver maintained that the Erckmann Experience was something no actor or technician could afford to miss. The bugs and demons could never get the better of anyone who had lived through it. Bysshe doubted if *he* could live through it. He needed toughening, not degutting.

At this point the prospect was of the remains of old vine terraces dropping to the service road among broom and bramble, and rocks like mammoth turtles slumbering in the grass. On a clear day the clobbered coast from Nice to Cannes could be seen. This morning nothing was visible beyond the slope of La Roquette. Bysshe came to a standstill.

It was feasible that Zwemmer had not allowed himself to be emotionally involved. Clinical detachment was essential to a doctor, and to live with lepers he would have to be a very cold fish. Otherwise he could drown in

26

pity and rot in the sights and smells. There was a difference between corruption and decay, between sweet drying and dying, and chemical regression to a basic mess.

The role of Zwemmer, whether as a feeling man or not, would require a very different performance from the kind Bysshe had brought to an art. He was not a deadpan actor; he used his face and had amassed a reliable stock of delusions, perversities and night thoughts with which to start the action. He had learned finesse. What he had in his eyes was an invaluable asset which could compound emotion with effect. Only at rare and culminating moments did he permit the hurt to be picked up by the rest of his face. One could overdo it. Carver's crack about the organ-grinder's monkey was relevant.

In any case, sensibility, which Zwemmer must have had, could hardly get past the facial hair which Zwemmer was known to have had. Only his eyes would be free to play their part. A lot would have to be conveyed by movement and arrested movement, by stillness, by stance. It would be a matter of timing and, of course, voice – inflection and accent. What sort of accent did Zwemmer have? There was so much Bysshe didn't know about him, he wasn't even sure if ignorance would help or hinder. A working knowledge could rate as preconceived notions. Erckmann would be looking at him, if he looked at all, to see if he would make up to his, Erckmann's, idea of Anatole Zwemmer. And what that was, precisely, God alone knew.

Bysshe could see the roof of Gluvas's shed through the olives. It was what was left of a vigneron's cabin, holed and greened by an ancient vine which still produced grapes of singular bitterness. 'Mon fort' Gluvas called the place. He seldom put in an appearance before noon, and frequently later.

Bysshe wondered if he should leave a note saying that he was going to the States. It would be months before he could come back to Ile-Marie, whether he got the part or whether he didn't. Having made the trip he would have to stay and take what was offered or what Carver could snatch: commercials, soap opera, porno flicks. Carver was of a desperate disposition where money was involved.

In the 'fort' Gluvas's machete, his gun and saw hung on the wall. His strength was here, the congenitally indolent man's cherished show of action. Round the string bed were assembled cider casks, above it hung bunches of onions.

The floor had not been swept for years. Whatever had been dropped, provided it was not wanted or to be used again, had been allowed to stay and congeal or petrify or wither. Bysshe stirred about with his foot. In a corner a hip bath was half full of sacks and goose feathers. A necklace hung on a nail, it was not a rosary, just the sort of thing, crudely carved and painted, on sale to tourists as 'fabriqué dans la région'. That was no lie, except that the region happened to be Korea – or Hong Kong.

Lacking pencil and paper, Bysshe considered tracing a message on the floor. But Gluvas would never notice changes in the grit. He went to the door of the cabin, put a hand on the lintel.

Framed in that rough entry he looks out at the native compound, the mud huts, pot-bellied children, the green maw of the jungle. Seeing – what?

The milk of human kindness? In Zwemmer's case it was surely cream. He would be seeing death, his own included, his past life and what he was missing in the way of career, women, games. Turning with a suddenness both warding and passionate, Bysshe addressed the string bed, the hip bath, 'You are my children' – it was the sort of thing a monolithic old man with a touch of God would say.

Erckmann would want music. He always wanted music. One of his spells relied on upsetting the applecart, especially the applecart of a storyline. There would be shots of unrelated but arguably metaphysical significance to break the continuity: a man dying, a woman undressing, a child skipping. Then the camera would switch to surf riders or an air balloon over English meadows, or a lion at its kill. With sound, he would employ snatches of flagrantly inappropriate music to

28

sharpen the moment on the screen, juxtaposing, and overlays of pop and classical. For Zwemmer it could be a Bach chorale and The Animals.

The orchard trees were covered with a painstaking scab, silver-grey, the same colour as the olives. Easy on the eye and mind, a non-grab colour. Restful. You could rest in it and dry in it and break, if you had to, like the twigs and seed-pods. Bysshe hoped not to break, but to harden and get himself a tegument for all seasons, all eventualities.

One might have supposed that at his time of life his psychic skin would have thickened along with his corporeal one. In fact it had thinned, which if he thought about it – as he did – was also supposable since he had less to commend him now.

The trees ended on the bleached slope of the Roquette. Walking down the hill he felt the metallic grasses clicking his bare ankles. On the lower slope, watered by hidden streams, there was green pasture, periwinkle, rockrose, mallow and wild orchids. It was where the geese liked to forage.

They were there now, they had heard him and were standing stock-still, looking up the hill. That they made no sound might mean that they recognized him. Or were holding their fire. They did that, they waited, not a feather stirring, even on the downy young ones, and then all together, stretched their necks and gave tongue.

He is a gaunt old man smelling of sickness, following the path beaten by the bare feet of the women who go down to wash in the river. He is deaf to the scream of parrots and the chattering of monkeys, he thinks not of his children, the lepers, but of the woman he has loved and left, the beautiful Viennese. She is married to an Austrian count, an important government official. They are Catholics, divorce is out of the question and she had noble, not to say high-stomached moral principles which even their passion could not overrule. Also there is her husband's career. They were forced to renounce their love and he had come to Africa to forget, and to atone for crimes which no moral principle had kept him from committing. But he cannot forget her and he knows that he smells not only of his children's sickness but of his own mortal sin. He is never alone at the hospital, but he is the loneliest man in Africa. He is going to the river to find solitude, to be free, at one remove, of the unending demands on him. The jungle waits, pandanus leaves as big as umbrellas, and giant lianas hanging in ropes.

Bysshe fingered the hair he might expect to have on lip and chin and over the disciplined nerves of his cheek.

On the bank of the river, the same river that he had travelled years ago on a little steamer which shrieked at every bend in the hundreds of miles of bends, the old man stands looking into the brown water. Something moves, slips away. A crocodile. He sees its unwinking malevolent eye going down into the smoking mud.

The geese, with an internal chuckle, moved away and began to clip the grass round the oieboy who was lying on his back among the periwinkle and mallow, as he often did. Bysshe had accepted that he must support layabouts – workers would not have suited him or his garden – but he wondered at the boy's indolence. It was not, as in Gluvas's case, sheer bloody disinclination. The reverse: there was expectancy in it, the boy was waiting. His body was spilled on the grass, prodigal – even profligate – of its youth which could only be spent and might with greater profit be squandered. He still had everything to lose. Bysshe felt a pang of resentment which only deepened when he asked himself what it was the boy waited for. What could he expect?

Through the overlarge jeans, split by someone else's patellas, shone the bones of his knees. His feet were planted soles down as if in a moment he would leap up on them. His chest rose and fell, softly, scrupulously expelling each breath. His fingers, curled into his palms, were the fingers of a child, cushion-tipped and tender, for all their scabbing and bruising. He appeared to be sleeping soundly. One eye was closed, the other showed its habitual glaucous streak beneath what was left of the lid. Bysshe had never been able to decide how much, if at all, he could see with it.

He sat on his heels beside him. He still felt a shock of disbelief whenever he looked into that face. Zwemmer could not have looked at anything much worse. Disbelief demanded that he look away, preferring not to believe what he saw.

One side of the face had been denaturized. What served as flesh was the colour of raw meat, an old rawness in which the blood had darkened and the living tissue had dried hard and rigid as wood. It was covered by a membrane of terrible flimsiness, thinner and more brittle than a beetle's wing, yet stretched mercilessly taut from brow to chin without a wrinkle or any provision for movement or variation of texture.

The mouth was badly scarred and healed short, catching up the corner into a permanent joyless rictus. The left eyelid, overburdened with scar tissue, hung low and half concealed the glimmer of something like a clouded jelly. In sleep, or the heat of the day, the boy had pushed back the hair from the fruitful side of his head, leaving an area of stitched-up skull. If he was aware of the state of his face as compared with other faces, he did not try to conceal it.

As Ewing had said, it was obscene. But the obscenity lay in the contrast between the halves: the pure half was mocked and forgotten. The crippled half mocked and was remembered.

Bysshe, when he remembered it, did so not in entirety nor as a worsening sequence. He had glimpses like flashes from a nerve end. As if he was being warned about something that was going to happen, or had happened, or ought to be stopped. He might have been alarmed, but recognized these glimpses as one of his ploys. His practice was to summon visions to help get an action going for the camera, and naturally – his nature being as loosely organized as anyone else's – visions could come unsummoned. And unproductive.

But this was his chance. He should touch the membrane which served as skin to cover what served as flesh. He should know the actual texture of mutilation. He needed to know it as a physical fact for himself. And for Zwemmer. And if he said for Zwemmer, he must say for Erckmann too.

He had a longing to break and relieve the stricture of the boy's cheek. But when he approached a finger to it, the geese advanced on him, hissing like a hostile audience.

2

'You know where they've gone.'
    'I didn't say so.'
    'You saw an address.'
    'It wasn't an address.'
    'So what was it?'
    'Why?'
She tries to stop things happening by asking why.
When we were in infants' school if she didn't know how
many beans made five or if someone was going to sit her
in a puddle she'd cry 'Why?' and open her eyes so wide it
was hurtful. She had round Muppet eyes then; now she
wears glasses and her eyes look poached.
    'They're our responsibility,' I said. 'Yours and mine.
We must go after them.'
    'I can't go and leave everything!'
Everything being pension Thursday, Tesco Friday,
Coronation Street Monday and Wednesday.
    'Tell me what it was you saw.'
    'It was what she'd written: "Hotel, grand place,
nice." "Where's this then", I said, "what's nice about
it?" and she ate the paper.'
    'She what?'
    'Oh, I don't know!'
To Darlene, ignorance is a commodity and she's
careful with it. Incomplete information tempts people to
put two and two together and do the work for her. Most
of the time she keeps herself in an adjustable twilight.

33

When things get too near the bone – her bone – she chooses total darkness and opts out.

I said, 'She watches too much television. She wouldn't have gone with him otherwise. He's not televisual, but the situation is.'

'It's been going on for months. I've seen her get droopier and droopier, weeping over the phone. She wets the receiver. I knew it was a man. I said to her ask him round, why don't you?'

'You must have known there was something wrong.' With a girl like Cherrimay everything could be wrong. I've known her weep because her half-moons weren't showing. 'Of course it was right for him. He's become a new man. There's only one Pike, so that just means a lot more of the old one. It was obvious to me what was going on. He's tried before, but he always comes back for his morals and I don't interfere unless my plans are upset. Of course I would have if I'd known it was your Cherrimay.'

'I keep asking myself why. Why couldn't it be some nice boy? She's seventeen years old and he's fifty if he's a day.'

'Forty-eight.'

'He's abducted her.'

'More likely she's abducted him.'

'You think it's funny. You don't give a damn how I feel!'

'Of course I do. But she's taking my place and I feel bound to ask what she's putting into it. The difference between her age and mine is a minus quantity so far as I'm concerned. There has to be something else, something more.'

'Anything I could do you could always do better!'

Darlene's let herself go. I'm big, but built to scale. Darlene's bones are lost in flab. Only her feet have stayed dainty – like pig's trotters. I said, 'You were better than any of us at ballet.'

'I had it in me to be a dancer. That wasn't enough for you, now it's my daughter who's not enough.' I hoped her heart was sound, it was jumping about in her throat. She cried, 'Not enough for what?' and I could see that she was drawing on something from way back. She can't help it, she hasn't advanced. Cherrimay, her daughter, has picked up the short change. They both open their eyes wide and see their own noses. I used to try to help Darlene with the school exams; I worked out a system of signals for her but she couldn't even remember what we'd arranged.

'You know,' I said, 'your French wasn't so hot, was it?'

'What's that got to do with it?'

'Are you sure the word was "nice" and not "Nice"? Could it have been the place, not the taste?'

'What word?'

'The word you saw on the paper, before Cherrimay ate it. Have you thought it could have been Nice, France?'

'Why should I?'

'It could be where they've gone.'

'Why would they go to France?'

'I wonder. Pike doesn't like Abroad. Perhaps it was her idea.'

'You think she started it? A girl just out of school chasing a man old enough to be her father? Or her grandfather!'

'Not grandfather. Pike didn't make an early enough start for that. I expect he got round her and she was flattered.' I had to work at my expectations, but they are, have been, maximum and private, whereas Darlene's are merely those of an outsider. 'He's still presentable when he's shaved and tidy. That's how I knew he was meeting someone. Not only did he have a bubble bath, he left off his thermal underpants and he wouldn't do that for snooker evenings.' I said, seeing Darlene's face, 'Don't worry, it would be for the purest possible motive. He'd want to be young all through for her.'

'It's disgusting!'

'It's human. Predictable. He's taken the car and his nylon shirts. If he's taken his passport I'll know where they've gone.'

'Where?'

'To Nice. Like in nephew.'

I know my way around Pike, where everything is in him and how it works, up to the point at which it works. He was given to me to know. I started studying him before we were married. I could write a book about him and it would make interesting reading if you like horrors.

I admit to being totally surprised by this affair, I could have been knocked down by a feather at there actually being an affair. For Pike to have a girl is contrary to all expectation – an expectation I've learned to live with. The refrain: blessed are they who expect nothing because they won't be disappointed, has also become my policy.

It's not true that there have been other women. He's picked up the general idea because it would be hard not to, but he can't put it into practice. I cover for us both: whatever may be seen to be wrong with my marriage it's not going to be that.

If he could run away with a girl, if he could believe there was a future in it, Cherrimay Pugh would do as well as any. In fact she would do better, being the daughter of my old schoolfriend, Darlene Lufkin that was, our near neighbour, and a source of information. Darlene leaks information droplet by droplet and you pool it to suit yourself. You have fun at someone's expense, only this time it would be at mine. Up to the point. Because in the circumstances no one was likely to question Pike's manhood. He had done me a part favour by taking Cherrimay Pugh.

If the words on that piece of paper which she ate had been in a different order – 'Nice hotel, grand place' for instance – I shouldn't have given it another thought. But 'Hotel, grand place, nice' didn't add up. You don't call a place nice if you've just called it grand. Besides, I remembered how Darlene used to entertain us in school when she conjugated French verbs with a Merseyside accent. So I took a chance on the address, that it *was* an address – like 'Hôtel du Grand Place, Nice'. I had nothing else to go on.

On the plane I had time to think. The hotel might

have another name, it might just have been described to Cherrimay as 'grand' and there might be more than one Grand Place, and hotels in all of them. Those two would hardly sign in as Mr and Mrs Pike. And they might already have left for somewhere else.

Where would Pike take a girl? Being scarcely able to believe he would take a girl anywhere, both widened and narrowed the field. They could be making for Spain or sitting on Southend pier.

By the time I was breaking the clingfoil off my lunch tray I couldn't believe any of it was happening to me. I suffered complete loss of credibility. Something to do with the altitude I suppose. I looked down at the sea and thought now that's not necessary, I could drown in one of Darlene's droplets.

Then after all, it was easy. I found a taxi at the airport and told the driver 'Grand Place'. He shrugged. I tried 'Hôtel du Grand Place', and off we went.

I'd been to Nice before. It's Abroad, banana trees and sunbrellas and wedding-cake buildings. I can take it or leave it. The cab pulled up in a narrow street alongside a huge new smoked-glass and steel block. The lower floor was full of agricultural machinery arranged on grass mats.

'Where are we?' There was no square and I couldn't see any hotel. The driver pointed. 'Chambres, douches, confort' was daubed on a wall. 'This is the Hôtel du Grand Place?' He nodded and put up the fingers of one hand, so I gave him five francs. He put them up again. He kept putting them up, and each time I gave him another five francs. Then he put up the fingers of both hands. I said, 'I don't know what you charge for a ride but I think you've been paid,' and picked up my bag and walked away. He shouted after me. I turned and looked at him. He exploded ten fingers, shut them into fists, beat on the steering wheel and drove off.

The street was one-way; it was too small to be anything else. The top storeys of the new block flamed in the sun, while the other buildings lurked at the bottom of a cut-glass canyon. They were old places with shutters and balconies, and I noticed shops selling wine, bread and video tapes. People were eating at tables on the pavement. Cemented into the walls were stone basins planted with geraniums. I didn't like the look of the hotel. It was tall and skinny and pocked, as if someone had dug pennies into the brickwork.

Inside I was met by the smell of garlic and French fries. That's all. There was nobody at the desk, and what I took to be damp on the walls turned out on closer inspection to be tapestries, old snail-coloured pictures of women in steeple hats draped over stags. The plumbing was hammering away in the depths, the place had seen its best days. Pike, I thought, is this your love nest?

I went to the desk, and prodded a cat sleeping on something which could be the hotel register. I needed to look at that, so I felt no qualms. The cat leapt up and arched its back. I got the book, turned it towards me, but couldn't read the writing which was mauve, spidery, and sloped backwards.

'Madame?'

She must have come from under the tapestry, a small blonde, heavily made-up. I'm blonde – I chose to be when my hair started to go streaky – but at least I don't paint. I've a nice skin, nothing to hide. Women who paint themselves are putting on a disguise and must have cause.

I said, 'This the Hôtel du Grand Place?' She nodded. 'Have you got someone here by the name of Pike?' She picked up the cat and cuddled it round her neck. 'Pike,' I said, tapping the register. The cat clawed its way over her shoulder. She took up the book and ran a blood-red nail down the page. 'English. Like me.'

She made her lips into a pink bud. 'Pew?'

The French language has to be mouthed, made a meal of, and I don't speak it unless I have to. 'P-I-K-E,' I spelled it for her.

'Non. Mais Monsieur et Madame Pew sont anglais.'

The penny dropped. Mr and Mrs Cherrimay Pugh. So she *had* brought him here to the 'grand place'. How had she managed it, what had she used? It could only be hope, which he has never lost. I tell him miracles don't happen, you are as you are.

'Have you got a room?'

'Une chambre?'

'Single.'

'Pour combien de personnes?' I held up one finger. 'Pour combien de temps?'

It was going to be a battle. She didn't care if I took a room or not. One of us had to be at a disadvantage, linguistically speaking, and it wasn't going to be me. 'For one night. Or longer. I don't know.'

'Voulez-vous voir la chambre?'

I knew I wouldn't like it, but there wasn't much choice. 'Which room are Mr and Mrs Pugh in?'

She took down a key. 'Par ici, s'il vous plaît, madame.' I thought she was going to take me to them.

She unlocked a door on the first landing. It was pitch dark inside the room. She went in and threw open the shutters. I saw a bed, a wardrobe and a washbasin with enough pipes for a church organ. So this was the accommodation being offered to me. 'Haven't you anything better?'

'Madame?'

I dropped my bag and went to the window. The view was into a sump full of barrels and fruit boxes. Looking up, I saw the blue old Riviera sky as if through the wrong end of a telescope. I suddenly felt sorry – and mad – for my poor Pike. It wasn't his fault, it was in his stars that not even this once could he get something right.

'Celle-ci est propre, tranquille, et très confortable. Peut-être madame désiré-t'elle quelque chose à un autre étage?'

She had got something wrong too: the measurements of the face she had painted over her own. The effect was too big and bright. I said, 'I'm here to get my husband.'

She didn't bat her false eyelashes but she knew what I'd said, she could speak our language. The idea was to make me speak hers.

'Je suis Madame Rosier,' she said.

'Mrs Pike.'

'Je vous assure qu'il n'y a personne ici de ce nom.'

'There is now,' I said.

*

39

My glance out of the window hadn't been inspiriting, but it had been informative. As I looked up between the walls to the sky I caught sight of a familiar and very personalized object. Seeing it in that foreign place brought the situation home to me. For the first time I saw what I was getting into – what I was being done out of. Pike's stars could queer things for me too.

Someone had told him once that germs generate on a wet face flannel, so he always dries his after use. At home he puts it in the airing cupboard. Here it was now, draped over the shutters of a room above. Not the sort of object to turn anyone on. It turned me into a fighting force. When Madame Rosier had gone, I checked the location on the floor above, left my bag and went up the stairs.

History was on every tread: spillages, cigarette burns, stiletto-heel holes. I took note of all of them because this was Pike's love nest. I knocked on a door, it was room 32, and had it turned out not to be theirs I would have tried the next one. And the next. But Cherrimay herself opened it to me. She took one look and her jaw dropped so low that I could have posted a small parcel in her mouth. 'So here you are,' I said. She made as if to close the door but I had taken the precaution of getting my foot in. 'Mr and Mrs Pugh.' What happened next was typical. It was the sort of thing Cherrimay did, and the sort of thing that happens to Pike. In that respect they were suited.

She flung wide her arms and started dodging in front of me as if keeping goal. I saw the goal over her shoulder – my husband, Pike, lying on the bed.

'You shan't!' she kept saying. 'You shan't!'

'Shan't what?'

She meant it as a general veto: she didn't want me to exist. But Dulcie Pike was here, and all Cherrimay Pugh could do about it was dissolve into tears. I said, 'Stop prancing about and stop crying. Nothing puts a man off like a messy weeper.' It was sound advice, but what I intended was to advise him about her and her wet nature. 'Pike, what's going on? What are you up to?'

'Nothing!' cried Cherrimay. I could believe that,

certainly, but I couldn't understand why they should come all this way to get up to it. It didn't make sense. 'He's ill!'

'Ill?'

'He's hurt his back. Can't you see?'

I took her by the shoulders and put her aside, though I would like to have put her out of the window. My husband, a roaring boy when in form, lay whimpering among the sheets. I asked him what it was all about.

'I've pulled a ligament.'

'The same one?' He got his back years ago and it's been a boon to him ever since.

'I think I've torn it.' That figured. Given the situation, he had to increase the odds; a mere strain wouldn't be enough to release him from his current obligations. I plumped myself down on the end of the bed. 'For Christ's sake, I'm in agony!'

'Don't swear.'

'That wasn't swearing, it was praying.'

'How did it happen?'

'The way these things do.'

'What way's that?'

'Does it matter?'

'There's one way that would matter a lot to me.'

I looked him in the eye and he had the grace to colour up. 'How the hell did you find us?'

'*That* doesn't matter.' I got up to take a look round the room. I was interested to see what he had brought with him, the only time in his life when he had had to pack for himself. For his second honeymoon. Perhaps he would call it his first. He is still capable of blaming me for the botch-up at Tossa de Mar, Spain.

His pyjamas were brand new, crisp blue poplin with a motif on the breast pocket. He had bought himself a dressing gown: at home he wears a cast-off of mine, when he wears anything. Pike in his striped pyjamas is a familiar sight to our neighbours on Sundays; he dresses when it's time to go to the local, and given a warm summer morning he washes the car in his night attire. He had brought the flight-bag, though they hadn't flown. This was the one we took to Majorca, stained by a

41

bottle of duty-free which had been smashed inside it. His brushes, which I hadn't missed so much as I missed their smell, strong and hairy – subconsciously I prepare to smell it as I approach our dressing table at home; the cuff links I gave him for Christmas, and of course that face flannel outside on the shutter. He had also brought his grandfather's watch with the bullet on the chain. Pike has a fixation about that watch, it's his link with the past. For him it *is* the past; he doesn't believe in the Wars of the Roses, Julius Caesar, or Henry the Eighth because he has nothing to show for them.

Her things were there too, her make-up stuff: lipstick, foundation, eyeliner, nail varnish and a little brush for her lashes. It really got to me, seeing them lying with his things on the dressing table.

The room was frowsty. They might not notice the stain on the carpet where the radiator leaked, and the veneer peeling off the wardrobe, but bliss would wear thin, I knew. If it hadn't already. 'What made you come here?'

'My pen friend recommended it,' declared Cherrimay.

'The French Riviera?' I looked at Pike.

'My pen friend used to work here in her school-holidays. Doing the bedrooms. She got us fixed up and the lady downstairs has been ever so kind. She fetched a doctor.'

'And what did he say?'

'We don't know,' said Pike. 'He stuck a needle in my backside and charged two hundred francs.'

I had to smile. No doctor can take Pike's back away from him.

Cherrimay knelt beside the bed and laid her head on his arm. 'He's coming again tomorrow.'

'A few more visits,' said Pike, 'and we'll have to go home.'

'Fine,' I said.

He looked at me, greenish round the gills. 'I'm not coming back to you.'

Cherrimay, Darlene's daughter, whom I had known as a baby wet at both ends – and so had he – put her arms round my husband with a protective gesture and looked at me, the brave little doe defying the wolf.

That did it. I took off my coat. I've said I'm big, I can loom, and I loomed over that bed. Their bed. Cherrimay shrank from me, tried to shrink into Pike, which caused him more pain than pleasure judging by the way he winced.

I rolled up my sleeves. 'Move over,' I said to Cherrimay.

'What are you going to do?'

'What I always do when he gets a bad back, gentle massage and manipulation.'

'Leave us alone,' said Pike.

'Anything that French doctor can do I can do better. For significantly fewer francs. Now move over!'

'You and me are finished, Dulcie. Have been for a long time.'

'What you mean is you never got started.' To Cherrimay I said, 'But that's my business. I contracted to cope, one way or another. Marriage is using what you're given, making the best of it. Sometimes making the best of the worst.'

She gazed up at me out of his arms. 'We love each other.'

For her that solved everything. I don't call it innocence, or ignorance, I call it dimness, under-endowment, and it's dangerous. Not to her, to everyone else. Especially to Pike. 'He's old enough to be your grand-daddy.'

'There's no telling you anything,' said Pike.

'There's no telling me *that*.' I plucked Cherrimay off the bed. She was pluckable, she came away in my hands. I rolled Pike over and he yelled like a baby. I stuck my thumbs into the small of his back.

'You're hurting him!'

'Did you bring a hot-water bottle?'

'Of course not.'

'Go and buy one. Buy two. Your love may keep him warm but his back needs toasting.' She stood there blinking. 'Go on,' I said, 'or would you rather spend your money on French doctors?'

43

She went reluctantly. Pike and I settled to our routine, me easing and coaxing his muscles, he whickering and burying his face in the pillow.

'You're making a mistake,' I said. 'Cherrimay Pugh's no good to you. I'd like to know why you thought she was.' He mumbled something. I pulled his pyjama trousers down to his knees and he begged for mercy. 'While we're on the subject, why did you come to Nice of all places? It's not your scene.'

'She had this address. And Webb-Ellis is buried here.'

'Who?'

'The man who invented rugger. He was the first to run with the ball.'

Everyone has something sacred. With Pike it's rugby football. He likes to believe he got his back playing scrum-half in his work's semi-final. I happen to know he did it slipping on something nasty outside Woolworth's.

Now Pike's back is an understood thing between us. It allows him to lead a free and active life when he wants to. For reasons best known to himself it 'flares up' from time to time. That's how he puts it: 'My back's flared up again.' There's nothing fiery about it though, it's a steady progression, from bad to worse, as required. It can be trusted to restrict and hamper and put him out of action if there's anything he can't or doesn't want to do. Obviously a godsend like that shouldn't start from a mess on the pavement, so it's been what you might call canonized.

That poor child, Cherrimay, hadn't a clue about any of this. She thought fate was against them. Perhaps she felt guilty and that she was being punished, and Pike's pain was part of her punishment. I wouldn't be surprised. But sooner or later it must become obvious, even to her, that there would be no idyll. She would realize that the most she could hope for was to be allowed to lie beside him on the bed and wipe his forehead and slip out occasionally to Uniprix to fetch him beer and pizzas.

I didn't sleep that night. There were people coming and going on the stairs, flushing the toilets, having

44

baths, conversations, quarrels, nightmares and telephone calls. It all seemed to be happening outside my
door. I got up once and looked out. A man and girl were
right outside. He was kneeling down fixing her girdle. It
shouldn't have been difficult because it was all she had
on. 'Stay calm,' he said to me – or something like it – in
French. I slammed the door and turned the key. I was
probably the only one alone in that place. Keeping
myself to myself. What for? *Who* for? I often used to ask
that question. Knowing the answer doesn't help me
now.

When I went up to their room next morning,
Cherrimay had locked me out. I waited a while, then
knocked. She called, 'Who's that?' I replied, 'La femme
de chambre, madame,' and she opened the door. 'Don't
do that again,' I said, 'or I'll have to ask for the master
key.'

'They won't give it to you!'

'If I tell them the facts they will.'

'What facts?'

'That my husband is ill and I have to attend to him.'

'He doesn't want you. He never has!'

'You're taking too much on yourself. Pike's my old
married man and what I don't know about him isn't
worth knowing.' Though it might be to her, because odd
scraps were all she was ever likely to know.

'You never even call him by his name!'

'Pike's his name. He's a big eater, like the fish.'

'You've never understood him.'

'Listen, childie –'

'I'm not a child, I'm a grown woman! And I'll tell you
what else I am –'

'Tell her nothing!' Pike had heaved himself on his
elbow. 'I'm sick of this!'

'I know what you are,' I said to Cherrimay. 'I've
watched you hold your breath with temper because
your mother wouldn't buy you jellybeans. And that was
only yesterday.'

'I'm not ashamed of being young, I'm glad, and
proud!' Cherrimay Pugh could be seen stretching up to
meet the occasion. 'I've got something you never had.

45

You're not his wife, there's a whole lot more to marriage than you've given him –'

'You surprise me.' I tapped Pike between his shoulder blades. 'Does she surprise you?'

'Go away and leave us alone.'

But by evening I had him out of his bed and sitting in a chair, though not without protest. There's no one like Pike for making himself heard. The day we married, my brother called him the 'loud baboon'. Of course I asked Doug what he was getting at. He said, 'The wedding-guest here beat his breast for he heard the loud baboon.' He'd been drinking and anyway he has a minimal alcohol threshold. But he was right.

I was well aware that Cherrimay was getting restive. The signs were unmistakable. My own feeling was that the ceiling had come down a few inches every time I went into that room. She roamed around it, twitching things, poking her finger through holes in the curtains, leaning out of the window to see the sky. I guessed she was trying to stop herself from wondering. By the afternoon I knew that I only had to wait for things to take their course – and there was only one course.

I even rang Darlene and told her I'd caught up with them. 'You needn't worry,' I said, 'she'll soon be home.' 'How do you know?' 'She's fed up with him. I can tell.'

I could have felt sorry for them individually, but those two together, those particular two, cancelled out my finer feelings. Cherrimay on her own was a chip off the old Darlene Lufkin block, no smarter, no prettier, and really no different from her mother, except that she had it all still to do. But with Pike, tied to him with a love knot, she had become the last person in the world. There was no pitying *that* combination. They were simply ludicrous.

However, there was no need to be bored whilst waiting. I went out, walked around the town, looked at shops, sat in the gardens where there were fountains and palm-trees and statues of Liberty, Equality and Fraternity. I avoided the usual Côte d'Azur attractions. I'm not a beach person, I don't take my clothes off and lie on the sand with the Kentucky fried chicken boxes. I didn't even go to look at the sea.

One thing I did find that cheered me: our old Escort parked near the hotel. It was thick with dust and scrawled with French words, no doubt insulting. But it looked viable and I was pleased. I'd be able to get about.

Next to the hotel was a café-bar called the Galerie des Lilas. There was barely room for two small tables and chairs on the pavement outside which meant that passers-by had to step into the road, but no one seemed to mind.

That first afternoon as I sat at one of the café tables I considered whether I was doing myself a disservice by keeping on with the massage and manipulation. There was a risk that Pike would get mobile before Cherrimay's patience ran out. On the other hand, he must be made to understand – they both must – that he was no good without me. If I say he's precious little good with me, that's my business. It's the choice I made thirty years ago, and even knowing what I know now, would make again. Where does that leave me? It leaves me with Pike.

It was hot and I was grateful for the shade and the cool at the bottom of this canyon of a street. I ordered tea which came in two bags hung in the pot like drowned mice.

At the other table were a boy and girl in their late teens. He wore shredded denim shorts, nothing else, and was the colour of teak, his skin glistening with sun-oil, which obviously gave the girl great pleasure. She ran her finger down his cheek to the muscle of his upper arm and back again. She was in pink satin trousers, poured into them, without a hitch or a crinkle. Over the tips of her breasts two rosebuds were held in position by an arrangement of silk straps. I expect a certain style of undress Abroad. Usually it's indecent or it's a positive eyesore. But these two were gloriously innocent, and what they were doing – claiming each other by touching, stroking, kissing eyelashes – was as green as Adam and Eve before the apple. It was what Cherrimay should be doing. Tied to Pike she was missing her greenness. She wouldn't even know she had had it, she'd dry up before her time. I hate to see anything wasted, especially on Pike.

When the waiter came they waved him away. They didn't want anything and he didn't insist. He stood in the doorway, arms folded, watching them. I watched too. It was quite an exhibition, a touching demonstration of tenderness. I have never been on the receiving or the giving end of anything like that. When I met Pike I was a fun-loving girl with a secret streak. I used to pray. Night and morning I knelt down – there was something I wanted and thought I shouldn't want. Daytimes I left my desk in the typists' pool and went to the staff toilet to ask for guidance. I enjoyed a joke if it was clean but I wouldn't hear God's name being taken in vain.

I told myself that Pike was the perfect man for me. He was happy and big, big-built, big-hearted, generous to a fault. Generosity is his fault. It's constitutional. Physically and mentally he's too big to concentrate. He's a roaring empty shell, as I found after we were married. And that's when I stopped praying. It didn't seem reasonable to ask God to undo His handiwork.

It's a pity about me. I have this streak which might be romance, or sex. It won't let me quite give up my expectations. Even now.

This boy at the café table took his girl's hand and nuzzled his way to the crook of her elbow. She stroked his hair. Then he sprang to his feet and brought her to hers with the same movement. Hand in hand they ran into the Hotel du Grand Place.

When I went up to room 32 for the evening massage session it was like an oven, the shutters were closed and Pike was face down on the bed with a hot-water bottle in the small of his back.

Cherrimay declared that he was better, but when I lifted his pyjama jacket the shape of the hot-water bottle was burned on him bright pink. 'You made it too hot,' I said.

Pike said, 'I thought you weren't coming,' and in the next breath, 'We don't need you.'

'You'll need a skin graft if she goes on like this. Don't

48

blame me if it hurts.' I started the massage.

He yelled into his pillow and Cherrimay rushed at me like a demented housefly. I swatted her with the hot-water bottle.

Pike has a nice back, broad shoulders, flat blades and a well-buttoned spine. He's broad in the beam but it all looks right. Each time I see his back I get a pang.

'I saw the car,' I said, 'and I'd like the keys.'

'What for?'

'To drive it.'

'Where to?'

'I want to call on my brother.'

'What brother?' said Cherrimay.

'Rex Snowdon, the film star.'

She knew that, everyone knows. It's a five-minute wonder. 'You're not!' people say. 'His sister? Never!' The men say, 'Pull the other one', and the women ask for details.

'We're twins,' I said. 'We happened to be born together.'

Certainly we never did anything else together. As children, told to run away and play, we ran in opposite directions. I played with bat and ball and skipping-rope, I liked action. Doug messed about with cigarette cards and beetles in matchboxes, very private. Sneaky, I said then.

Pike turned his face up from his pillow. 'He's in America.'

'He's here, at his villa in the hills.'

Cherrimay said, 'Does he look like you?'

'Hardly. He's the beauty of the family. Girls flock to him like moths to a candle and if they don't get burned they drop in the grease.' My fingers were leaving white weals on Pike's inflamed skin. 'It's easy come, easy go with Doug.' He went through a bad patch in his teens, I was the better-looking one then. He grew too fast, he had boils on his neck and he knocked out his front teeth in a motor-bike accident. 'He has what it takes.' I laid my palms very gently on the weals on Pike's back. I believe if I gave my mind to it I could develop the healing touch.

49

'He never comes to see you,' said Cherrimay.

'What would a man like him, leading the life he does, do in Sidcup?'

'What life?'

'Mixing with film and TV personalities, directors, oil millionaires, Presidents – he did a film with Ronald Reagan once – he owns a ranch-house and a swimming pool, he runs half a dozen cars and a chauffeur. When he gives parties he hires a firm of caterers and the parties go on for days.'

'He gets in takeaway food,' said Pike.

'Doug makes more from one film than anyone I know makes in five years.'

'And spends it.'

'Why not? He doesn't owe us.' When our parents were alive he sent them a cheque every Christmas. It was too much for them to spend or to talk about and they used to put the cheque away and try to ignore it. When we asked if they'd heard from Doug, my mother would say, 'He always writes,' and show us the typed envelope. All he'd written was his name on the cheque. After they died, we found uncashed cheques to the value of five thousand pounds in a biscuit tin. 'My brother's a free agent, not like some of these show people, married and divorced several times and paying fortunes in alimony.'

'Why isn't he married?'

'Because he's queer,' said Pike. 'He has to be, to do the things he does in front of an audience.'

'What things?'

'A real man wouldn't be able to stop himself.'

That was wonderful, coming from Pike. 'Jealousy is natural,' I said. 'Doug has his pick of the beauties of stage and screen. He may not be real, actors seldom are, but he's man enough.' It used to upset my mother, seeing magazine pictures of him draped round half-naked women. I used to tell her that it was a publicity stunt, deny his promiscuity; it was what people expected of him and of every film star. I remember how she would fold her thumbs under her pinafore and say she supposed so and go on living somewhere else in some other time.

'How do you know he's here?'

I saw that Cherrimay was getting interested. The situation she was in, anything would be interesting. 'I read an article in the paper. It said he's living at his villa in the South of France. Hiding.'

'Why?'

'If anyone knows the film business, when to be available and when to be hard to get, he does.'

'The car's like me,' said Pike. 'Out of action. If you want to see your brother you'll have to take a taxi.'

'What's wrong with the car?'

He rolled over. I know his face like the back of my hand, but he introduces some funny wrinkles sometimes. 'Let's get this understood, Dulcie. We don't need you, we don't want you. You can't turn back the clock. You ought never to have come here. Be sensible and go home.'

'Can she massage your back?'

'She does better than that, she keeps it warm. In bed we're as cosy as a banana and a banana skin.'

I'm not given to visions, but I had one then. Pike disgusts me not for what he is, but for what he isn't. I went to the basin and washed my hands. The last thing I would be able to bear was to take his smell with me to that room downstairs. Those two watched, Pike open-mouthed, having said his say. Each time he opens his mouth he thinks he'll win.

I rolled down my sleeves and buttoned my cuffs. On the dressing table I'd seen the ignition key among Pike's loose change and her back-combings. I picked it up and put it in my handbag. 'I'll take the car to a garage and get it fixed.'

Pike forgot himself so far as to swing his legs off the bed. His feet touched the floor, but then his knees gave way and he fell. I left Cherrimay draped over him – just like a discarded banana skin.

I could find nothing wrong with the car. It was reluctant to start but it often is, and it had been standing idle for days. I ran the engine, engaged gear and inched to and fro. A plastic bottle burst under the back wheel. The gauge showed an almost empty tank. I switched off, locked and walked away.

My clothes were sticking to me and I decided to have my breakfast outside, at the café. The lover-girl sat alone at one of the tables, waiting for the loving to begin. Or continue. This morning she had on a see-through garment, everything could be seen through it. Personally I believe some things should be left to the imagination. As I didn't fancy witnessing love-play so early in the day I sat at the other table with my back to her.

Cherrimay Pugh, the chosen, the chooser, of my husband, looked none too fresh that morning. She appeared in the hotel entrance carrying the flight-bag. I beckoned her over. She frowned, but came nonetheless. 'Are you leaving?' I asked her.

'I'm going to get something for lunch.'

'What did you give him yesterday?'

'Why?'

'There's a connection between what he eats and what he suffers.'

'We had crab sandwiches and apricot tart.'

'Was that wise?' She fiddled with her hair. I don't think she'd washed, her face was smudgy and half rubbed out. I said, 'It's no diet for a man in his situation.'

'What situation?'

'Why, lying in bed all day, taking no exercise. Crab's binding, it's a well-known fact. So is pastry. He has problems with his bowels. He's not all that young, you know, he shouldn't take chances.'

'I'm not a chance, I'm a certainty.'

Cherrimay had sent that back like returning a ball. Obviously she was learning. Her face sharpened and her Muppet eyes, the same as Darlene's when she was young, turned gooseberry-grey.

'Well,' I said cheerfully, 'that being so, you want him on his feet as soon as possible. Proper food will help, improper food will hinder. Get him an underdone steak with chips. A green salad – lettuce, cucumber, watercress – there's iron in watercress – and fresh fruit, apples and oranges. No bananas.' I smiled, but of course she didn't. 'And milk – there's calcium in milk – it's better for him than tinned beer.' Pike hates milk, with luck he'd throw it at her. 'Go to the supermarket and pick out the best stuff.'

'I can't speak French.'

'You don't have to; just help yourself and pay at the cash-out like we do at home.'

'He doesn't like me to be away long.'

'I'll take you in the car.'

She sat down suddenly. 'Is Rex Snowdon really your twin brother?'

Aha, I thought, but not laughing. It had been on her mind, and still was. 'Yes, but we're not identical, he's altogether different from me. A different personality. Of course film people live in another world.' I sighed, playing at being fuddy old Dulcie admiring her glamorous brother. 'He's got a wonderful place up in the hills, sauna, sun lounge, patio, swimming pool.' When I was there he'd had a puddle on the kitchen floor.

'But he's old.'

'He's younger than Pike. I'm younger than Pike.'

She stared past me. It was sinking in, I thought. Then she said sharply, 'That's disgusting!'

'By two years – not thirty.'

'Those two are carrying on as if they're in bed.'

I realized that she was talking about what she could see over my shoulder, the young sweethearts at the next table. 'Oh, I don't know,' I said. 'They're in love.'

'You call that love?'

'They're on their honeymoon.'

'I don't want to watch that sort of thing in the street.'

'But you wouldn't object if you were the girl and he was the only boy in the world.'

'You call him a boy?'

'In years. You can't call Pike a man in anything.'

'What do you mean?'

'You must know by now. If he tells you that what he does in bed is all there is, don't believe him. You're being cheated.'

'What of?'

'Your birthright. Every woman's born with the right

to full and happy sex. You could say she's born out of it.'

'I don't know what you're talking about.'

'I'm talking about what matters to a normal woman.'

'You needn't worry about me then!'

Darlene used to be like that, bold as a balloon one minute and the next tearful and deflated.

The couple from the other table passed us as they went into the hotel. He held her to him with a hand thrust under the waistband of her see-through trousers, his fingers could be seen between her thighs. And he wasn't the one she had been with yesterday. He wasn't a boy, he was paunchy and bald and had a Mafia face.

'She's a common prostitute and I call it disgusting!'

I admit to being disappointed. My sentimental streak leaves me open to it. I said, 'You only have to look at Madame Rosier to know the sort of place she's running.'

'Give me the key of the car.' Cherrimay held out her hand without a please or a would you mind.

'It's our car, mine as much as his. I'm going to Ile-Marie this afternoon. You ought to come with me.'

'Why?'

'It's not every day you get the chance to meet a famous film star. And it's bad for you to be confined to that room all day. I suppose Pike wouldn't let you come.'

She stood up and looked down her nose. 'I do whatever I want and I don't want to come.'

'I'll be leaving at two o'clock.'

I waited till half-past. It was stiflingly hot, but I sat in the car like a chicken in the oven in case she changed her mind. I was hoping she would. I had no plan, I had to play it as it came and every time I peeled her off Pike's back it came my way; a little win for me.

When it was obvious that she wasn't coming, I asked myself, not for the first time, what kept her with him. What keeps a girl, any half way to normal girl in her busty teens, with a non-event like Pike? I knew what she could see in him but surely by now she'd seen that it wasn't there.

How long had it taken *me*? In terms of time, four days.

Our honeymoon was less than half over when my doubts crystallized. I tried again and again, ardent young wife as I was longing to be, to dissolve them. They dribbled slightly, but at the core they remained rock-hard. Petrified. In terms of emotion – faith, hope and charity – it took longer. Viability a human being must have, it's what makes the being human and I'm reluctant to rule it out in anybody. And I was most of all reluctant to rule it out in my husband. That's why I followed him to Nice.

The car had its front wheel jammed against the kerb. I fought with the clutch and accelerator to get it out. Then I crept it along to a garage which I had located nearby, filled up with petrol and had them check the oil, battery and tyre pressure. Finally I rumbled off, the car picking up courage, or resignation, and some speed.

I can't say I like the way they drive Abroad. It's one place where you're sure of being chased, whatever your sex, age, or vehicle. I know my capabilities and I try to suit them to the car. But anything on wheels was on the autoroute that day: cars from A to Z, caravans, tankers, juggernauts, dodgems, Japanese fire-eaters and animals – lions, tigers, elephants and monkeys in cages on a string of trailers. A clown waved from the back of a truck. He was in full circus rig, white face, bottle-nose, ginger wig and check plusfours. The whole lot swept by, that road's a circus anyway. I pulled into the backlash behind the last truck and overtook a French car which was wallowing about in the middle lane.

After the N7 I turned off on a D road, one of those which are yellow and wormy on the map. They go to godforsaken places like Doug's. I had a very general notion where it was, the one and only time I'd been to it was years ago, by taxi from the airport. I was picking up the signposts, climbing high, then dropping, then the road pushed into pine woods. There were glimpses of sea and mountains in the distance and glasshouses winking in the valleys. I passed through a village where they were having a saint's day and had to wait behind an army of little girls dressed as drum majorettes, blowing whistles and beating biscuit tins. I asked some bystanders the way to Ile-Marie. They pointed onward and slapped the back of the car as if it were an obstinate cow.

After that the country got wilder, with gorse bushes and fireweed and rustic berger-bars like in deepest Surrey. The road doubled and re-doubled. I would have missed the turning to Ile-Marie if a goat hadn't run out of it in front of my wheels and scrambled up the bank.

I swung on to a narrow road where bushes and branches reached out and swiped at the car, a place where the natural world was taking back this little macadam strip. I remembered Doug saying something about it being a secondary road, used only by locals. He said it was impassable in the spring, melting snow came down from the hills and made it a raging torrent. It occurred to me that he was showing off because we live in Sidcup.

I passed some isolated villages and a wayside shrine – probably Marie's – and a man breaking stones in a ditch. Then the ground opened out, I left the trees, and what had started as a rock-strewn common became a green meadow, spiked with rushes. We're there, I said to myself, I remember this bit.

I didn't remember the next, however: a wall topped with broken glass and under it pits full of bramble and thistles. A track led into the trees, there was a gate knitted up with barbed wire. A board nailed on a tree said 'Propriété privée, défense d'entrer'. No name, no pack drill, but I got the meaning.

When I think he makes a big living pretending to the world, I have to ask myself who started it. The answer is the aunts and uncles and grandparents and cousins and schoolteachers and, of course, my mother. And my father. Because he let them take Doug over, left him with them when he should have knocked out the kinks and steered him into a proper job. Doug was good at drawing, he could have been a draughtsman. He read encyclopedias, he could have been a teacher. He read the medical dictionary, he could have been a doctor. He's got this knack – I don't call it talent – for making himself out to be what he isn't.

Its finally taken him over. A wall with glass splinters on top and a barbed wire gate are the permanent things he has to show for years of fooling and they're to keep people out, after he's made his money by bringing people in.

I left the car and went to the gate. The padlock was unfastened and hung on its chain. There wasn't a sound, which was remarkable, because if nothing else there are always insects cracking away, rubbing their legs together, I'm told, something British beetles do without fuss. The air smelt like a hot mince pie. I pushed at the gate. Half of it moved a little then stuck on a clump of daisies. The bolt of the other half was jammed in its shaft, I had to kick it to release it. The screech of those hinges set my teeth on edge, I'm sensitive to sounds; being a singer with perfect musical pitch, a noise like that does me an injury. But it's typical of Doug, he's always been able to upset me without trying.

I hadn't seen him since he turned up at father's graveside in a floppy panama with a red and green band, a linen suit and spotted cravat. I caught him trying to sneak away afterwards and asked him where he'd got the hat. He said it was the only one he could find and he'd worn it as a mark of respect. Whereupon I reminded him about black armbands.

I wasn't anticipating seeing that hat again, but suddenly it was there, on the other side of the gate. It took me right back to the day of the funeral, seeing the mud waiting to be shovelled on my father. He was the only one who had time for me. Everyone loved Doug because he was so pretty. Dad used to say, 'He takes after your mother. You and me are a different breed, Dulcie.' He didn't smile when he said it; he was a plain man, plain-spoken. And I didn't mind being like him.

But it wasn't Doug on the other side of the gate, it was a tall old man wearing the floppy panama which had been present at my father's graveside, the same red and green band, the self same pimple on top, a personal affront to the dead. The man had a hook knife in his hand. He had been cutting grass, the blade was stained green and from the look of him it might be stained another colour any moment. I said, 'That hat belongs to my brother.'

57

He lifted the knife and swung it to and fro. I was close enough to feel a breeze. I looked him in the eye, not a pleasing experience because his whites were yellow and the middles like black bullets. 'Let me pass, please.'

He said something, in fact he said a lot and took trouble saying it. I had to suppose he was speaking French but it might have been Arabic. He exploded words at me, I was reasonably sure he was being offensive.

'I'm Rex Snowdon's sister. His soeur. Compris?' I made as if to get by him. He made as if chopping the air, and spat. Some of his personal juice landed on my dress which was a nice one, put on specially for Doug.

I snatched off his hat and threw it away. My mind doesn't desert me at such moments. I act on the spur and follow through, 'I'll have you sacked,' I promised him. But Doug's not loyal. Would you expect him to be, a man who dresses like a gigolo for a solemn family occasion?

The old man cursed. Blasphemy sounds the same in any language. He was torn between shutting the gate on me and going after his hat. It had fallen in front of the car, which gave me an idea. I got in and started the engine. I turned the front wheels on the hat, revved and moved forward. The old man left the gate and ran. I let him snatch the hat from under the wheels and then I drove in. He threw his billhook. That I did run over. If it's cut the tyres, I thought, I'll make Doug pay.

The track was terrible, flints and upended bricks, but I had to drive fast to get away from Father Time. I thought if I don't get a puncture I'll break an axle. Either way, my little brother – nervy, secretive and cold as a fish, hiding himself back of beyond in Shangri-la or Mon Repos or whatever he calls this place – would have to pay.

The track plunged between walls of rock. I scraped my near wing, hitting the mirror and clipping it to the side of the car. I couldn't see if I was being followed. The rocks were like huge cheeses, roundly stacked and chipped to show creamy pink under brown rinds. The car bounced and bucked, any minute I could hit a cheese and I knew it wouldn't be creamy.

Then the track opened out and I was running under olive trees. Beyond, to my left, the ground dropped away, in fact it stopped in midair because there was a lot of shagged blue haze and no solids. The track took a sharp right bend; and luckily so did I. It went uphill and had been roughly cobbled by someone with a thing about cars. I went into heavy-duty gear and roared through the trees. Doug must have heard me coming.

I stopped over a patch of oil stains in the only space between bushes of strapping great flowers like trumpets. As I turned off the engine I seemed to turn on the heat. It threatened to cook me. I'm a big woman, womanly, my flesh melts on occasions: too much sun is one occasion I like least.

The last – and first – time I had seen Doug's house was before he moved in. It was more or less a ruin and I couldn't tell that it was any less now, but you'd have thought he would have smartened the place up. I'd have thought he would have pulled it down and built a nice bungalow if he was so smitten with the situation. Why he should be, though, I'll never know. There was no view; to see the coast he would have had to chop down the olives and everything that was getting beside itself. Distance lends enchantment, so it might have been worth it.

Except for the roof which had been retiled, and a new front door, the house looked much as it did years ago. Not a lick of paint anywhere, the shutters bleached and peeling, and the walls which had been white were grey except round the stack pipes where they were green. The dome – yes, there was a dome to top it all – was smothered with bougainvillea.

I called 'Doug!' But the shutters remained closed. They would be, to keep out the heat, and I longed to have them keeping it from me while I drank a cup of tea. I was going to make sure I didn't get the boiled straw-water he had given me last time, rosemary tea he said it was.

'Doug!' With all this alfresco living I didn't reckon to have to knock on the door. He would be somewhere here, flat on his back, Sleeping Beauty. 'Doug!' I called as I pushed into the jungle: with the sort of spell that was on that place it wouldn't require a hundred years to truss my little brother up like a fly in a spider's web.

I came across one of those luxury swing beds, with canopy and fringe, and sat in it for a breather. 'Doug!' If he was within a mile he must have heard.

So must the old man with the knife. I'm not fanciful, but if overexposed I get the creeps. Nature does that to me; it's so messy. I never liked Sunday-school treats because they were invariably in the country or at the seaside. And here everything was out of proportion, threatening: the butterflies big as birds and the weeds shoulder-high.

I tried the front door, then I went round to the back of the house. There was some still life – a bin overflowing with empty bottles, grapefruit and avocado skins, yellow newspapers, and plenty of movement – swarms of flies and lizards going into cracks in the wall. I tried the back door. It was locked, but the window shutters were open and I looked into the kitchen. I had seen it before Doug moved in: all easy-clean stone, stone walls, floor, sink, and a veined marble dresser which Doug said was for home butchery. It looked like a morgue then, though I've never been in one, and it didn't look cheerful now. There were dishes in the sink and a tap dripping on them making a crater in the grease. I'm hypersensitive to mess.

Obviously the film star wasn't at home. But Father Time was, and probably coming for me with his scythe at this very moment. I had knocked off his hat and I wouldn't put it past him to reciprocate with my head.

I pushed on, meaning to do a circuit of the house before going back to the car. I trod on a yoghurt carton, it went off like a pistol shot and someone laughed. I assumed it was laughter but it was more of a cackle, an old man's cackle and still some way off.

I was hotter than I had any business to be; and the dripping tap made me realize how thirsty I was. A cup of tea would have been nectar. I had come to the end of a path and a kind of cave under the rock. It looked cool and turned out to be quite tidy, not all over itself like the rest of the place. There was a trickle of water coming from a pipe and filling a natural basin on ground level. The ground had once been tiled and recently washed over, revealing what was left of the pattern. In the rock were two niches: in one was propped a mirror, in the other a black and gold flask. I took it down, it was empty, but smelled expensive. One of Doug's whims was to come here for a bath, I supposed. Or was it where Father Time did his toilet and had run out of aftershave?

The water in the basin was amber colour, the coolness reached out to me. I knelt down and put my hand in, then my arm. I didn't disturb so much as a grain of mud, and the water was so soft it didn't feel wet. I put my other arm in, and there I was, enjoying myself, up to my elbows in water that could have come from anywhere. A cup of tea couldn't have been more refreshing. For two pins or less I'd have dipped right into the pool without stopping to take my clothes off. There was something special about it, about the grotto or cave or whatever, and I was so pleased with myself, with being myself and being there, that I leaned down until my face was touching the water. I wanted to get into that cool, amber colour.

I know now that what I saw in the pool was what made it special. At the time it gave me a terrible jolt. One minute I was looking into restful water, the next I was looking at a devil.

I believe in devils, I just hope never to see one – they do well enough without showing up in the flesh. But I saw one then. His reflection was as solid as mine, amber-coloured, and quaking with the movement of the water. No one should look like that, not even a devil. There are limits, the ugliest creature has reason for its ugliness – snouts for snuffing, buck teeth for biting, scabs for putting off other biters, or as marks of war. But to screw up and throw away a face is not reasonable.

It took me a full minute to get myself together and realize that it must be the current distorting reflections, mine included. I scrambled to my feet and swung round. There was nobody in sight, just the grasses shaking.

Madame Rosier had it in her to be a professional snoop,

paid to report other people's business. But she hadn't fully understood that discretion is part of the job. She must have risen at dawn to put on her face. Once I got up to look out of my window – I couldn't sleep in that place – and there she was, down in the yard among the empty bottles. It was barely daylight, but she showed up like a traffic-signal: green eye shadow, red lipstick, orange scorchmarks on her cheekbones.

Whenever I glimpsed her in the passage at the hotel she'd remove herself so fast I'd be left with her colours on my eyeballs, as if I'd been looking at the sun.

There was plenty of snooping potential at the Grand Place: couples coming and going – no luggage: single men with document cases – I asked myself what documents? And girls with prix fixée written all over them. There were older women in pearls and eye-veils and one with a moustache and size nine slingbacks, some sort of specialist I daresay. I never felt easy there, though I kept myself to myself and Madame R. had no opportunity to find anything out about me. Or so I thought. Then when I went up to Pike's room one morning there she was.

I never liked that room. To Pike it was the Garden of Eden. When I saw Madame R. there I felt I'd come face to face with the serpent.

Pike was on his back, smiling his patient smile. Those two women, Cherrimay at his feet, stroking his hammertoes, and Madame R. holding her elbows and showing stop, wait, go, were encouraging him to make the maximum fool of himself. It's a classic situation and I don't like to see it. I'm not a man-hater, men have a certain superiority and I like to see it respected.

I was still getting a jolt every time I saw Pike and Cherrimay together, but I could handle it now. Finding Madame Rosier with them shook me up again. I suppose I was seeing for the first time how it could look to people who weren't involved and didn't know the first thing about us. She was the last one I would want to know, but it struck me forcibly then that the three of them had been having me over.

'What's she doing here?' I said straight out. She

pretends not to understand English and that can work both ways.

'This lady called to ask how I am,' said Pike.

'What did you tell her?'

'That I'm as well as can be expected with a damaged spine.'

He can be bold, can Pike; with support, even cocky. Especially with female support – it was me gave him his faith in the opposite sex. Sensing that I'd have to be careful I said, 'I'll soon have you moving.'

'No – don't touch me.'

It must be some sort of subconscious joke when a man with no backbone chooses to have a bad back as a general excuse.

I rolled up my sleeves and went to the bed. Pike sat up, without a wince or a moan, and put up his fists – the gallant welterweight fighting back from the floor.

I said, 'What's this?'

'You do me no good, in fact you do harm, you manipulate all the wrong things. Rubbing me up the wrong way is what you've always done!'

I turned to Madame Rosier. 'You a qualified masseuse? All part of the job?'

'When I think what he's suffered,' mourned Cherrimay. 'You banging and slapping and grinding his poor bones!'

I said, 'It's like kneading dough, you knock it down to make it rise.'

'I'll never let you hurt him again –'

Madame Rosier murmured something. I said, 'She understands more than you think and I don't intend to discuss my business in front of her.'

'There's nothing to discuss,' said Pike.

Madame Rosier uttered a hiss and snaked across the room. At the door she let go her elbows, inclined her head, and was gone.

'We can't afford to upset her,' said Pike.

'There's such a lot you can't afford.'

'We've got everything we want.'

'We've got something you never had!' cried Cherrimay.

63

'How would you know what I had?'

'I know what you didn't have. So there!' She really did say it – so there! – and only just didn't stick out her tongue.

'You're easily pleased,' I said. 'Having no standards, you would be. That's one thing you've got in common with him, and it's just as well because you'll have to get used to doing without.'

'We don't need money to be happy!'

I knew then that it was going to be all right, I even felt sorry for Pike.

'Dulcie, I know how you feel –' that's what he used to say in bed when he hadn't the remotest notion how I felt – 'it's come as a shock. I wanted to tell you, I tried to tell you, but I couldn't find the words. There was no way to break it gently.'

No way to get me blinking back the tears, murmuring 'I won't try to hold you', grateful for having had my share of him and ready to stand aside and give someone else a turn. I went to the door, opened it and looked along the passage. 'Does she talk English to you?'

'Who?'

'Madame Rosy.'

'Well we don't talk French,' said Cherrimay, sounding affronted. 'She's very nice, she's going to get us an electro-massager. We can hire it by the hour.'

'It'll release you,' said Pike.

'For what?'

'You needn't feel you've got to stay. I'll be on my feet in no time.'

'You can go home,' said Cherrimay.

'Don't think I'm ungrateful. It's not your fault our marriage didn't work, God knows you tried –'

'Oh, He knows,' I said.

'I did too, morning, noon and night. I tried too hard and stopped my natural reflexes.'

'Especially at night.'

Pike's face lacks any hardening ingredient but it gets thoroughly basic so that you see his ground plan.

'It wasn't dignified, chasing after us,' said Cherrimay. 'My mother would never have done it.'

I gave her a look of mild surprise. 'Wouldn't she have chased after your father?'

Then Pike came up with his thought for the day: 'We're not compatible, you and me, we're chalk and cheese.' It was all I needed.

'I wonder what that makes you?' I said to Cherrimay. I was getting tired of the long slow take, I could see the end, and I wanted to get to it. 'Aren't you sick of being in this room? A young girl like you should be living your own life.'

'I *am* living it.'

'We'll soon be able to get out of here,' said Pike.

'Give us back the key of the car!'

Young people nowadays don't ask, they demand, and not even as if they're doing you a favour, but as if you're doing them a *dis*favour by obliging them to speak to you at all. If she'd said, 'May we have the key?' if she'd said 'Please', I'd have thought about it. I don't know what I'd have decided because of course while I had the key I had them. But as it was her bad manners decided me. 'I'll keep it for now. Doug wants me to go to see him again. And I'd like to. It's another world up there. You can relax, forget your problems, get away from yourself. It's something to do with the isolation, being cut off from the rest of humanity, and of course that's a lot to do with money.' It takes money even to keep that place dropping to bits.

'Why didn't you stay there then?' said Cherrimay.

'I wouldn't like to leave you just yet. Later on, perhaps. I'll need to keep the car, but I promise not to go until you're able to get about by bus.'

'What did I tell you?' cried Cherrimay.

What indeed? I would have been interested to know what Cherrimay Pugh could tell my husband about me. I sighed. 'Nice to be rich, not just comfortably off, but loaded – like Americans.'

'Doug's not American.'

'His money is.'

'It's not your car,' said Cherrimay.

'When we married, Pike endowed me with all his wordly goods till death did us part. Of course I'll drive you anywhere you want to go. Let me know when you feel like an outing.'

'This is good enough for us,' said Pike. 'It doesn't matter where we are so long as we're together. Cherrimay's the part of me that's been missing all my life. I didn't even know I ought to have it. You wouldn't understand, I don't understand it myself, it's the way I am.'

This was the same Pike, eating his cake and having it. 'It may be the way you are,' I said, 'but what about her?'

'I'm all right! Aren't I?' She ogled Pike: her mother while she remained unspoken for had rolled her eyes at everything in trousers. With Darlene it had been more automatic than promiscuous.

'Well then,' I said, 'as you're so snug and happy you won't mind me having the car.'

The look that passed between them started out electric from Cherrimay but got bogged down in Pike's low wattage. She bounced off the bed. She had the energy, she was the one who would set the springs a-twangling. She'd soon find out that there's nothing much only one can do.

'We paid to bring that car here!'

'Till Friday,' I said, 'or Saturday. I'll keep it till the weekend. By the way, how long are you planning to deprive me of it? I'll want it at home.'

Cherrimay started prancing again, flinging out her arms and dodging in front of me. 'Make her give it back!' She wasn't learning. Pike lay there on the bed, white and greasy as if he'd dropped off a spoon. I recalled how long it had taken *me* to learn. I had to have the first lesson over and over again, I couldn't accept it. I was full of trust, and I blamed myself, I thought Fate was testing me and through me, him. I thought we were being given a dummyrun of life together.

'You're looking puffy,' I said to her. 'You remind me of your mother and you shouldn't. Not yet.' She stopped prancing and turned a deep garden pink. With youth in her favour she was like a cabbage rose. 'When she was carrying you, Darlene put on air. We thought she'd float away. Remember?' I said to Pike. 'Us putting a pound's worth of coppers in her pocket to weigh her down?'

And he said, Pike the astonisher, Pike the obscure: 'If you're going to see Doug tomorrow why don't you take Cherrimay with you for the ride?'

'I don't want to go!'

'I've been thinking, I'm being selfish.'

'You're not!'

'Keeping you with me all the time is asking for trouble.'

'What trouble?'

'You could get tired of it.'

'I'll never get tired of you.'

It wasn't quite what he had said, but he had to take the shift in meaning: after all, he is forty-eight years old. 'I'm responsible for you, I'd never forgive myself if anything went wrong.'

'What could go wrong?'

'What indeed?' I said. 'At her age everything ticks. You're fussing over her like a father. Is that what she wants?' She looked from me to him and burst out laughing. I said, 'It's well known that girls tend to fall in love with their dads.'

Pike said, 'She'll be glad to go with you.'

Cherrimay stopped laughing and started to cry.

I missed the daily chore of waking Pike. He has to be fetched back to consciousness. It's like a rebirth, I've brought him into the world every morning for thirty years.

I was starting the day at the Hôtel du Grand Place with a sense of loss. It showed me that I needed to know my blessings before I could count them.

I was down in the street next morning while they were hosing the gutters. Our car doesn't like wet underneath. We have trouble on wet days. I've told Pike whoever heard of a car that won't go in the rain? He says it's my imagination, although imagination is one thing I don't cultivate, there's enough going on without me adding to it. Pike puts his hand into the engine and fumbles it, my method is to sit in the driver's seat and pull and push everything. I get results with the right combination of

67

choke, parking lights and Radio Four.

Driving off at last I forgot about keeping to the right of the road and found myself facing a taxi. I shot past and left him climbing all over his cab. What's with these people? There's only a strip of water between us and them, but they're *foreign*. No balance. And Nice isn't real, it's like the old Crystal Palace, all hairy palms and fountains.

Doug could have bought himself some place in England, in Sussex where our father's father came from. Stage and radio stars – Naunton Wayne and the Crazy Gang – built themselves lovely houses on the Kingston Gorse at Ferring-on-Sea. But Doug has to be different. He works at it. I've watched him stop himself doing what comes naturally. He does the opposite, upside down, inside out, bad for good, black for white, tit for tat. He took up acting, because it's against his grain, and he chose to settle in another country, as near as he could to his own, without living in it. But I understand that, as far as I can understand anything about him. People don't change, they just get more like they are.

I stopped at a café. A wind was blowing and the waiter was pegging down the plastic tablecloths. I went inside. The place was empty. The waiter served me and then stood in the doorway tapping his teeth.

They make good coffee in France. Everyone has a gift for something: my father used to say mine was an extra special one, but he wouldn't say what it was. He said if you know you've got a gift you're liable to misuse it.

While I was drinking my coffee, I wondered what I was doing there. It's a question I don't normally ask myself because at any given time I know what I'm doing. Fundamentally I was there to get Pike back: sitting in an empty café listening to a waiter tapping his teeth and the wind flapping the tablecloths was part of it. And I wasn't going to see my brother, because he's one of the half dozen last people I'd go up a mountain for, so much as to be seen going, to give to Pike and Cherrimay Pugh the idea, plus gall, that my glamorous film-star brother wanted to see *me*. This was one of those times when every little counts.

As I left the café the waiter had to stop teeth-tapping and chase a metal menu-holder which a gust of wind sent bowling down the road. Currents of grit were crossing each other, the air was khaki colour, as were the pink geraniums they go in for over there – bowls and showers of them everywhere. No place looks the same without sun and sun is about all they've got that we haven't, on a regular basis, anyway. When it goes in, there's just the smell of Ambre Solaire.

The sky worsened as I drove, clotting up like a bad egg. Every bit of plastic, sunbrellas, awnings, flapped and swelled, a Pris-Unic bag spread itself over my windscreen. Dust came into the car through the places usually reserved for the rain. It came in farther than the rain, it reached down my cleavage and under my tongue.

I remembered the old man in the hat, Doug's hat, Doug's old man. Doug turns himself upside down, inside out, but he's no different from me. He's ordinary, like the rest of us. Ours is an ordinary family. Grandfather kept a sweetshop and father kept pigeons; they were good plain men and you wouldn't need a crowd to pass them in. We were brought up without fuss, we ate our greens and potatoes as soon as we were on solids, and went to the primary school when we could manage the toilet. But Doug has chosen to live in a mess when he could have anything he wanted.

I could handle old Papa Time, but there was going to be the wall and the barbed wire. If the gate was locked I couldn't see myself waiting for it to open. I once queued for a film of Doug's and was so annoyed with myself for queuing that I walked away when I got to the box office. At least if I didn't get in this time there would be no need to mention it to Pike and Cherrimay. It's loyal not to talk about your family failings.

Up there where Doug lives, the only let or hindrance to the wind are trees, the wall, and that gate which was open, dragging its padlock to and fro. I remember Doug telling me about the wind. He said it was known to have flash-cooked a goat and people in concrete tower blocks in the towns had to stay out of doors to avoid being roasted alive. I said why live in such a place. He said there were other advantages and smiled the smile he uses on the screen. It's supposed to melt women.

This same wind was burning my breath and blowing dust into my bosoms and led me to put the same question: what was I doing there? It was the second time of asking and the last answer was stretching it a bit. Going half way up a French alp in a grit storm to get Pike back? Could he be said to have got away? He was having a male menopausal symptom: trust him to have the symptom without the sex, and when it passed, he would have no option but to come back to me. I could be just wasting my time.

I might have gone further: asked if I could be wasting it because what else was there to do with it. But I don't encourage morbid thoughts.

I pushed back the gate and drove into Doug's private mess. The wind was whacking at the alfalfa grass, it had torn down a vine and was turning it like a skipping-rope. Upstairs a shutter had broken loose and was battering to and fro. For all the liveliness of the place there was no sign of life.

I leaned out of the car and shouted: Doug had to be up and about, he was a light sleeper and he'd never sleep through banging shutters. I left the car and walked up to the house.

The last time I saw Doug he was showing our age. It was at the funeral. I saw that he was getting heavy round the jaw, he had bags under his eyes, and some red threads. That's because he drinks too much, eats too much, generally overdoes it. He has women, but I can't pronounce on that, because I wouldn't know how much sex is too much.

Having made up my mind that I was about to see him again I was vexed not to. 'Doug!' My voice bounced back. I shouted 'Rex Snowdon!' Then I started coughing. A grass seed or an insect had slipped down my throat.

I struggled on toward the house. I'm shortwinded, I need all the breath I can get and I wasn't breathing. I thought, I'm choking on a grass seed – one of Doug's. It was one way of dying.

I made it to the kitchen door. The door was locked. I beat my fists on it and that took the last of my wind. I could see the dishes still in the sink, the tap still dripping, and I couldn't get to it. I had to have water to clear my throat. Then I remembered the grotto, the amber water, and my legs took me to it, my last breath was in my legs.

Someone was there, with his back to me, a naked back, a boy's, judging by the big shoulder blades. His jeans hung from his hipbones. He was busy at the mirror propped against the rock wall, turning his head this way and that, sticking up his chin, tucking it down again. Fancying himself. He took his face in his hands and held it to the glass, perhaps he was kissing his reflection. I didn't wait to see. I wasn't interested in him at that moment in time, though it was coming up fast to the moment when I would be.

He was between me and the rock pool. I pushed him aside, scooped up water and drank out of my hand. The water tasted sweetish. I scooped up another handful. It may have been that the water washed the grass seed out of my gullet or it may have been the shock to my system that shifted it. I think it was mostly shock, because it stalled a few other bodily functions. My blood froze and after a big jump so did my nervous impulses. I stopped coughing.

The fancier had turned round, I was looking him full in the face. Full, but you couldn't call it whole. He would be about sixteen years old, but you can't put a time to something you don't recognize. One side of his face, the left side, was no age. It was no face. Just a piece of raw meat like the meat on butchers' hooks, purple over the bone and dried up, the sort of cut you wouldn't buy. He had something that passed for an eye, though I couldn't pass it, and a puckered-up slit like a drawstring purse. All that was bad enough, but it stopped on a line from his forehead to his chin; no merging, no blending, one skin-cell dead and rotten, the next one to it living and sweating. The right side was all right, eye, nose, mouth perfectly formed – they used to call that sort of lip a Cupid's Bow till Cupid went out of fashion – half a perfect face.

I realized I'd seen the other half yesterday reflected in

71

the water I had just been drinking. But I wasn't prepared to see it again, and the two halves together really shook me. Putting the worst alongside angel's delight is the sort of thing Nature does all the time. But I did ask God why He allowed this. The answer came: for the same reason as devils are allowed in church, to keep our ends in sight, so we remember where we come from as well as where we hope to go.

'Hullo,' I said.

His eye was blue, any girl would have envied his blue eye and his eyelashes. His hair was the sort of Afro shower the youngsters cultivate, though his was naturally curly and yellow as a guinea. A guinea would be that colour, soft and valuable-looking.

'Sorry I shoved you.' His eye was on me, his good eye, blue and blank as a doll's. 'I had a coughing fit, almost choked. I had to get a drink of water.' The eye narrowed, if it saw me it was with suspicion. I said, 'You must have heard me' – if he hadn't been so busy with the mirror. 'What were you looking at?' I was needled, and anyway it was best to treat him as normal. 'Look,' I moved closer, putting myself into his field of vision, 'I'm here to see Rex Snowdon. I'm his sister.' Of course he couldn't understand. And I thought if he's the gardener it could be why there's no garden.

All at once I was angry, with the wind and the shutter still banging and with Doug and Pike. And myself. Not this boy. It struck me that his face was complete because other people show you a bit, then switch off and show another bit, never the whole picture.

'You're a proper little Jekyll and Hyde.' Something moved under a tuck of flesh, something bright. Something was looking at me, we were having a conversation. 'What's your name? Jekyll was a better man than Hyde, but it doesn't matter to me.'

He took a breath and let it out of his Cupid's lip: the other, the drawstring, tightened. He may have been sighing.

'You've got an interesting face. You're interested in it, aren't you?'

He exploded, seemed to break up, burst apart.

72

Without a sound. I got the impression he was laughing. I got it from his stomach which kept filling and half-emptying the waistband of his trousers. It must have been what they mean by a belly laugh.

'I'm glad you can see the funny side.' I *was* glad, he didn't have much going for him. 'It's been nice talking to you, I'm going to find my brother now.'

I looked for my bag which I had dropped somewhere. He moved faster and got to it first. I held out my hand. He folded his arms. 'Give me my bag, please.'

It bothered me, seeing it against his chest. He had a broad chest, hairless and brown as a nut. His arms were folded over my handbag, squeezing it to his square breasts. It made me breathless.

'Look -' I had yet to see his Jekyll eye look at anything - 'if you're thinking of stealing my money, don't. I'll call my brother, he'll call the police, and if you don't mind me saying so, you won't make a good impression.'

What he had going for him was youth, strength, and no moral tone. I went close, I thought at best he's only a boy and he's not the best of that. In case he hadn't understood, I tried to pull his arms apart. 'Give me my property!'

I wish I could remember what happened next. I've tried to play the whole thing back, I've gone over it again and again. It's clear up to the moment when I touched him. I touched him with anger, that I do know. I was ready to hit him, next minute to hate him. But that minute didn't come, there was a split in time, and I was taken right out of myself. By that I mean what I've made of myself, Dulcie Bysshe as was, Dulcie Pike as now is. I realized what was happening but not that I ought to stop it. That required a mental process and I wasn't having mental processes. I was having a brain and blood storm combined.

I *need* to know how it happened, and in detail. I need the details because I'm living with it, it's personal history and altogether too personal. Anger's not enough, anger should have put me off. I don't want reason, I want a let-out. Because one minute I was defying him,

73

the bag-snatcher, and the next I was where my bag had been, in his arms, against his chest. And I was kissing him on both sides of his mouth. I must have done, I must have put my lips to that cobbled-up slit. It turns my stomach to think of it. I kissed his soft Jekyll cheek and that other, the Hyde side – bone under baked skin. It was what I'd been wanting to do, I took the half a chance to do it, and there was nothing would have stopped me.

I had on my nice dress for Doug. It's very soft silk, this boy spread his hand and moved it up and down my back, getting the feel. His fingertips were rough, they dragged, but nothing would have made me stop him.

I didn't think this is wrong or this is right. I have no thoughts to fall back on now. I have all those feelings which I prefer not to remember. They're mine insofar as I have a system which is capable of them. To that extent I'm responsible. So is the boy. And so, ultimately, is Pike – because Pike's system is not capable.

Nothing could have stopped me. Except the boy. The boy got scared – as well he might – of what he was doing and what he had already done. He suddenly slipped under my arms. He was a gentle mover, anyone else would have thrown me aside, regardless of my state, thinking only of his own. He went, leaving my bag at my feet.

Crying's not common with me. At my father's funeral the cleaning woman cried and I couldn't even get started.

I was ready to drop. I sank down on the edge of the stone basin and blubbered into the water. When I tried to wash away the tears I made a thorough mess of myself. I couldn't face Doug after that. I drove back to Pike.

I remember once asking my mother where children came from. She was rolling pastry at the time and said their mothers made them. I said how, and she said with sugar and spice and all things nice. Even at five years of age that sort of thing infuriated me. I said why had she made two of us at once – it was what I was really after. She finished off her tart and trimmed round the dish with a knife. 'Because I had some bits left over.' Then she scraped up the pastry and made me a doll with currant eyes. I don't think she meant me to draw the obvious conclusion. She wouldn't think I was able to. But when the pastry man came out of the oven I bit his legs off.

Later I collected pictures of the reigning boxing and tennis champions. I put them on the walls of my bedroom. The men were beginning to wear those very short shorts and I wasn't particular where I stuck the pins. Doug tried to make out that meant something, and asked why didn't I like men. I said I'd love a man when I found one.

The only reason I can think of for remembering those days is that I had started to wonder just what bits had been left over. To make me. I've always been pretty sure of myself; I know what to expect, give or take a quirk or two. This episode was more of a bomb than a quirk but I was going to have to take it.

Mummy, I said, my feeling is it's one of your leftovers. You kept it for me. You decided it wasn't for your Dougie, he had to be nice throughout. It'll do for Dulcie, you thought; the chances are she'll never know she's got it. Sugar and spice for Doug, puppy dogs' tails for her.

I was flopped on my bed at the hotel, heavy as lead, empty as a glove. Genuinely exhausted. I kept dozing off, silly ideas came into my head, and sillier dreams. It was an unhealthy way to spend a morning. And that was an unhealthy room, the furniture cheap old stuff hanging on long after it should have been chopped up. Twenty thousand mosquitoes had been swatted on the walls, and whoever puts velvet curtains in a bedroom is making it nice for bugs. But no other way to spend that morning sprang readily to mind. The wind was howling and what I could see of the sky was the colour of ironmould.

I dreamed I was shooting Doug's hat. It was perched on top of a pole, I had a gun and I fired bang into the crown. The hat bled. I woke to hear knocking on my door.

Pike was the last person I was expecting to see in the flesh just then. When I opened the door and saw him there everything came back to normal. Here was Pike standing before me, the way he always stands, as if he's been kicked from behind. He stood at the altar like that the day we were married, sagging at the knees. It was one of the things I had meant to change.

'So you're up and about,' I said. I was glad to see he was still the same, Cherrimay Pugh's love hadn't been able to change him. 'How are you feeling?'

'I think I'll have to wear a corset.'

'I'll lend you mine.'

'I've got an inarticulate spine. That's what the doc said.'

'The French one?'

'The one I saw before we came away.'

'To check if you'd be up to Cherrimay? That was thoughtful.'

'God, I must sit down!'

He lumbered into the room and lowered himself on to my bed. 'I can't stand, I can't walk, I can't hardly sit. What's to become of me?'

'A vegetable.'

'You've got no feeling.'

'You've got too much. Stop feeling sorry for yourself.'

He blinked. 'In actual matter of fact I'm pleased for myself.'

People think it's easy dealing with a fool. But a fool has the advantage of not being bound by commonsense. The great thing is to keep your temper. It took me a long time to learn that. I used to wallow in my rage, while Pike got sillier and sillier. Now I disconnect. I look at his foolery as I would a bit of junk before throwing it out. What worries me is that when I'm old and dried up I'll have a dead seam where hope and charity should have been. 'Were you thinking of making a life with her?'

'Making a life?' He looked alarmed.

'Living together.'

'Yes.'

'Well then,' I said, 'the difference between living with her and living with me – and it's the only one so far as you're concerned – is that I won't let you be a vegetable.'

'Cherrimay and me are meant for each other. To think I nearly lost her that time when Darlene wanted to go and live up North –'

'When Cherrimay was still in her pram.' I tried hindsight, seeing them together, Pike and Baby Pugh, him dancing her on his knees, helping her toddle. I remembered him turning away when she grizzled. She was fat, sluggish and leaky. 'Are you telling me you fancied her then?'

'Age does matter,' he said, not giving me a glimmer of a smile. 'It matters a lot. She makes me feel young – so I can have life over again. I know I missed a lot the first time round.'

'Like what?'

'I take pleasure in her pleasure.'

'I don't mean to be unkind –' I think if you do mean to be, it should be in a good cause and not just for spite – 'but what pleasure can she find shut in with you all day?' My cause was to show him the trouble he was laying up for himself. Besides, I needed to know what they made do with, the two of them, in Madame Rosy's grotty back room. I needed it for when I woke at night, and the times when I couldn't bear myself.

I was hoping – how long does hope last? – for a short answer, like 'We hold hands', 'I tickle her feet'. But Pike put his hands over his face and spoke out of his palms, muffled. I think he said he was sorry. It's the sort of thing he would say, late and much better never. I could have killed him. I came close enough to it as to be answerable for the crime: only the action was missing. I could have done it with my bare hands.

'Look,' I said, 'you don't apologize for short-changing when you've been doing it for thirty years.'

'It wasn't all my fault. Nor all yours. We just didn't – we couldn't. Some people, some things, don't mix. Oil and water don't, it's a fact of nature. That's all.' When his brain is working he blinks, his eyelids take the strain. 'There are some substances which are harmless in themselves and poisonous together.'

'Is that what we are? Poisonous?'

'We couldn't know how it would be.'

'I know how it was. Exactly.'

'It's over. For you and me it's all over.'

I'll say this for Pike, you won't come across any streak of native cunning, he's bull-silly all through. But I felt

77

that if I lost my temper I'd end up crying, and in a queer sort of way it would be carrying on from where I left off in the grotto at Doug's. I couldn't have that, so I kept a grip on myself. 'And now you're going to put it all behind you and start a brand new life by starting in on hers. That's handy.'

'We love each other.'

'Does she know what she's letting herself in for?'

'Yes.'

When Pike's definite, he stands on the burning deck, about to go down for the umpteenth time, and ten to one he'll never know it. But this was one time when he would have to know.

'So,' I said briskly, as if it was settled, 'what are you going to do?'

'Get away from here. We only meant to stay overnight. Then my back flared up. It's been expensive. The fact is, we're short of money.'

'You'll have to come home.'

'No.'

On the burning deck, trying not to notice that his feet are getting hot. 'Everything comes down to money. Even love's middle-aged dream.'

'I suppose you told Doug about us.'

'Some things I don't tell to anyone. Do you think I want to broadcast the fact that my husband has left me for a schoolgirl?' Of course Pike's always been jealous of Doug's success with women, he'd want him to know about Cherrimay.

'In some ways she's grown up.'

'What ways would that be?' Shame is not in Pike's nature, when he blushes it's for other reasons. But he makes a thorough job of it, I've seen when he's been stark naked and little pink paddies have rushed all over him.

'What I mean is, she's not a child.'

'God knows what she is. He made her, so He must know.'

'We can't leave until we've paid the bill.'

'That's usual.'

'We can't pay. The doctor and the massager cost a packet. I'm skint.'

78

'Even I wouldn't expect you to expect me to lend you the money.' But I could see he was expecting just that.

'Do you think she'd take an IOU?'

'Madame Rosy? Let me know when you ask her, I'd like to be there.'

'Could I get a loan from the bank?'

'You could try the British Consul. They'll be bound to ask what you're doing here.'

'Doing?'

'You needn't say you're here for a grubby weekend. But they'd find out, through official channels. I doubt if they'd help.'

'What am I going to do?'

'Try sneaking away at night when there's no one about.'

'They're about all night long.'

'I've noticed.'

'At home I could get it out of the slot.' I forbore to mention that he would first need to have it in the slot, he can overlook essential detail better than anyone. 'God, what a country!' He sat on my bed cupping his buttock bones, one to each hand. 'I'll never get better here. They call this the sunny South and you could stew an onion in these rooms.'

'They already have, judging by the smell.'

'What the hell am I going to do?'

'Get away, you said when I asked. I certainly think you should.' He groaned, fondling his bones as if they were soft fruit. 'Look,' I began, 'when all's said and done – but don't think it has been yet – you're my husband and I'm the only one who can get you out of this trouble.'

'Yes.'

That was Pike, the everlasting Pike, handing me back my responsibility. 'So I'll settle your bill.'

'Dulcie, I'll pay it back, I swear I will, it'll only be a loan until I'm on my feet again –'

'And I'll drive you home.'

'We're not going home.'

'Not we,' I said, 'you. I'm not driving that girl anywhere.'

'You think I'd go back without her?'

79

'She can fly. I'll take her as far as the airport.'

'We've got no money for a ticket –'

'I'll telephone Darlene, she can pay the other end.' I didn't know if she could and I didn't care.

Pike started shouting. I don't pay too much attention when he shouts, I let what sense there is blow over me, rhubarb noise. Of course those two would get together again at home, but if I broke them up now the next break would come easier. And sooner.

He got up shouting that he wouldn't part from her. Then he seemed to get an almighty kick from behind and collapsed over the bed.

'Suit yourself,' I said. 'Stay with her or come with me.'

'Christ – I can't move –'

I must say he gets himself into some odd situations: he was doubled over my bed as if waiting to be spanked.

'Help me – do something!'

I looked at his big soft bottom and was tempted. My hairbrush was on the dressing table, it's a heavy one and has strong bristles. I could have given him a new sensation and it might have helped. They say one pain cancels out another.

'Get me a hot towel –'

'Where would I get such a thing?'

'For God's sake, Dulcie, I'm in agony!'

I went into the shower room, turned on the tap and soaked a towel. I took it to him still dripping. 'What's it to be?' I pushed the towel into the small of his back. He swore as the water ran down into his trousers. 'Are you staying here with her or coming with me?'

'She's frightened of flying –'

'Everybody's frightened of flying.'

'Why can't she come in the car?'

'I have a forgiving nature, but I'm not prepared to drive across France with you two billing and cooing in the back.'

His face opened to cry like a baby's. 'What am I going to tell her?'

'Tell her we'll be leaving first thing tomorrow.' I felt it was all coming my way, and I shoved the wet towel down into the seat of his trousers.

*

She got him by being thirty years younger than me, no virtue, no merit. Losing him isn't the end of the world for her, she'll forget him in a week. For me he's the way of life I've worked at ever since we were married. I'd like to have been a fly on the wall when he told her.

But little girls have no conscience, they want their own way and don't care how they get it. Cherrimay would put on a show – one big burst followed by a steady leak, then she would twist his arm. She would twist anything if it helped.

After he'd gone I looked out of my window at his flannel hooked on their shutter and tried to get a fly's eye view of what was happening up there. Then I gave up and went and rang Darlene.

'It's over,' I told her. 'They're coming home.'

'I'm just going out shopping –'

'Don't worry, you'll be back by the time they arrive. And they won't be together. I'm bringing Pike, she'll have to come on her own.'

'Why?'

'Because I won't play gooseberry.'

'How do you know it's over?'

'They've got no money, they have to come home.'

'What are you going to do? You'll have to divorce him –'

'We can't continue this conversation on the telephone. Your daughter's penniless, send her her fare or buy her a ticket at your end.'

'What?'

'If you want to see Cherrimay again you'll have to pay. She's not my responsibility and it's not in my interest to have her within a hundred miles of Pike. I've told you the situation and I'm going to ring off. This call's costing me money.'

'I don't know what to do!'

'Ring the Citizens' Advice Bureau.' I hung up, feeling pleased with myself. Pike's natural drawbacks include lack of money and I thought it was a neat move to use a risen situation rather than create one.

I stood myself lunch at a place where the waiter pulled out my chair and brought a bottle of wine in a bucket.

He made such a ceremony, wiping and displaying the bottle, that I decided to try it. It was sour to my taste, but I drank it down with veal cutlets and a peach tart. When I left, the waiter gave me a red rose. He was being paid for it of course, and for the way he watched me poke it down the front of my dress – as if he would like to have done it himself.

I went to the bank and changed travellers' cheques to pay the bills and buy petrol. I was looking forward to the drive and now that I was leaving I felt charitably inclined towards the place. I walked down to the front for a look round. The sea was on the other side of the fancy palaces and palms and didn't declare itself with that white gap in the sky which advertises our sea at home. I nearly missed it. It was the colour of weak coffee, and a few people were trying to have fun in the dregs. The wind screwed the palm trees and hunted torn paper and empty cartons and geranium heads. Everything looked scraped. I went back to the hotel.

I stood at the window of my room looking up at Pike's flannel with the dried germs on it and was sickened. I'd been that all along. Of course you can't localize a sick feeling, what I felt took in Pike and the girl, but didn't stop with them. At that particular moment I was sick of everything, including myself. And angry that sickness was getting the better of me. To take my mind off it I thought I'd get the car filled up and checked for the journey. I looked for the ignition key. It wasn't on the table or the bed, it wasn't in my purse or my pocket. I looked under the bed and in the bed. The wine I had drunk was making me very aware; I had a clear mental picture of the key and key ring lying where I had tossed it. I even heard the clink, muted, because it had landed somewhere soft. On the bed. When I came back from Doug's I threw everything down, myself included, on the bed. Pike could have picked up the key ring. He had the opportunity while I was fetching the towel.

Pike the opportunist. He wouldn't have registered the key ring until he sat on it; in his case opportunity has to do more than knock. I searched the room, then I went out to where I had left our car. That was gone too.

I blamed myself. I know all about Pike but not so much about Cherrimay Pugh. Coming to me to borrow money could have been a blind, a way of getting into my room and she could have put him up to that. My carelessness had done the rest. Even Pike will look to see what's sticking in his bottom. They could be packed and gone already.

I went back to the hotel and straight up to their room. And there was Madame Rosy in the act of letting herself in. She tried to shut the door in my face. We struggled. I'm bigger than she is, I got my knee in, then my hip. I broke her hold and pushed her in backwards.

One glance was enough. Their things were still scattered all over the place. I went in and sat down. Madame Rosy came after me.

'I have every right to be in this room,' I said.

'Monsieur and Madame Pew –'

'Mister Pike's my husband. She's nothing.'

'Madame, if you please.' She was at the door, signalling stop, ready, go.

'I'm stopping.' I had seen his passport on the bedside table. I picked it up. 'Here's his name – Pike. I am his wife.'

'Madame Brochet?'

'Pike. I keep telling you. I am Mrs Dulcie Pike.'

'This is not your room.'

'You're so right it isn't. I wouldn't leave a dog kennel in this state. I wouldn't stay in your hotel anyway. But for what those two are up to it's very suitable. Know what I mean? Dirty.'

She came on full current then, really lit up. 'I shall speak to Monsieur Pew –'

'He knows what I think.'

'If you do not go I must shut you in.'

'Suit yourself.'

She said something in her language, bit it up and spat the bits at me. Then she marched out and slammed the door. I was suited. I had to wait for them to come back and I was doing them a favour by keeping Madame Rosy out. She had come to snoop.

I didn't bargain – I should have – for Pike's mark. It's

a sort of spoiling: he roughs and generally messes up wherever he goes and whatever he touches. This room had turned into Pike country. Nobody wrecks the bed and strangles clothes and moults over the furniture like he does. Nobody can twist the toothpaste and get shaving cream on the taps like he can.

I picked up her nightdress, one of those Baby Doll efforts. And she had a drawer full of seethrough undies. On top was the pink bow tie he wears because someone once said it makes him look like Frank Muir.

I've said I'm not imaginative, I have to see to believe. What those two do together doesn't worry me, they can't do much. But seeing their things together, side by side, on top of each other, that gave me pain. I'm funny that way.

But not vindictive. At least I wasn't until I found the rabbit. Under the bedclothes. A blue nylon rabbit made in Korea, with red plastic eyes and reinforced ears. It was at least three feet long and smelled of Pike. It had been in their bed, it had her smell on it too, so I picked it up by the ears and threw it out of the window. It fell in the yard among the empties.

I had to wait a long time before they came back. Any time would have been long. It wasn't just the matter of his things mixing with hers: those two had spread themselves and I couldn't separate them from each other or from the room. Pike and Cherrimay Pugh were like jam, over everything, while my pain was low down. Gynaecological they call women's troubles.

Madame Rosy warned him, of course. When he opened the door of their room he was holding up his functions. When he does that, he looks fit to burst.

'Relax,' I said. I worry about his arteries. I worry about them seizing up and not letting his trickle of blood through. 'That was clever, the way you got the key of the car.'

He stared at me, blinking, swallowing, putting two and two together. He reached a decision – I saw it go down his neck to his arm – and pushed the door wide. 'You needn't stay.'

'Where's Cherrimay?'

'In the car.'

'Aren't you the one that needs to stay?' When he moved from the door it slammed, shutting us in. 'There's a little matter of an unpaid bill.' He reached under the bed and dragged out the flight-bag, stuck over with old tour labels. He started taking up things and pushing them into it: dresses of hers were bundled round shoes, black beetle-killers of his. I laughed. 'Packing, are you?' Everything from the dressing table – brushes, make-up, creams, aspirins, hair-combings, powder-spill, cotton-wool buds, dust, and their passports were swept into the bag. 'I could have taken a bet on how you pack.'

'I wish to God I'd never seen this place.'

'God sent you here to show you what a fool you're making of yourself.' Her nightdress was balled up with his dirty underwear – to see Pike packing is to witness an act of gross indecency. I said, 'You've got the car but what will you do for money?'

'I'm taking Cherrimay home.'

'Who's going to pay your bill?' He stood blinking and thinking – still thinking that I would pay. 'Not a penny,' I said. 'Not a Frankie or a Johnny, whatever they call their money. You don't think she'll let you get away without paying, do you?'

'She's pregnant.'

'Who is? Madame Rosy?'

'Cherrimay.'

'She's what?'

'She's going to have a baby.' That was Pike, spelling it out. At last. For me. For himself.

'Well,' I said, 'well,' while everything fell down round me with a sneaky little noise. And yet it was predictable, and totally logical. Cherrimay Pugh would start a baby with less ado than I would make about starting a batter pudding. And she was doing it early. 'You don't suppose it's yours, do you?' (I could see he did.) 'My God –' who else should I call on? Pike is God's mystery, mine not to reason why. Though I do. I'm as I was created, in the human condition, I was given certain thoughts and

85

certain feelings – oh very certain – and given Pike, what am I supposed to do? – 'Nothing's sacred to girls of her age, least of all their own selves.' If you're going to be unkind it ought to be in a good cause. '*You* didn't get her pregnant. Oh, she'll say you did and you'd like to think you did. Any man would.' Pike longs to be any man, he lives in hope. I could say he lives on trust because that's how people take him. Men and women. He looks, sounds, smells and acts like a man in all but one respect. As his wife I'm well placed to know what that respect is. 'Don't worry, I'll get the truth.'

'She's in no condition to talk, to you or anyone. She's shocked and upset, she can't stop crying. I don't know what to do, what to say to her. I don't know how bad it is, what harm's been done.'

'Harm? Is she bothered about losing her virginity?'

'Christ, I don't know anything!'

I admit to being sorry for him. He goes to bits in a crisis, in little fraught moments like when the frying pan goes on fire. And when he's stranded Abroad. 'What's the hurry?'

He was blundering round the room as if he meant to pack the furniture. What had happened to his back? One pain cancels out another.

'I've got to get her home!'

It seemed a good idea. In England Darlene could take over. He zipped up the bag, gave a last look round, as you do when you're all packed and ready to go. But he hadn't looked in the wardrobe or the chest of drawers and I knew for a fact that she had a suitcase with her, a white plastic thing still under the bed. 'Don't forget your flannel.'

There was something else he wanted to say. He blinked hard. I prepared myself for something wide of the mark.

'That man whose mother was frightened by an elephant –'

'What?'

'The elephant man. He was born like it because his mother was attacked by an elephant while he was in the womb.'

I got some surprise hearing him use that word. It's a bit technical and Biblical for him, so I supposed he had picked it up from her. After five minutes pregnancy Cherrimay would be into details.

I got some more surprise when he said, 'It really happened, didn't it? He was born a monster, it was an actual matter of fact.'

It was so wide of the mark I could scarcely stop myself from laughing in his face. But I did stop myself because I could see he was seriously frightened. 'Old wives' tales,' I said. 'How could a man look like an elephant? A parrot, maybe, or a monkey. Some people look like that anyway. If Cherrimay has a baby with a big nose it won't be because she's seen an elephant.'

'I blame your brother!'

'Doug? What's he got to do with it?'

'You've been to his place, you must know what goes on.'

'Goes on?'

'You've seen the company he keeps. I know what film people are, but he's got something running loose up there that ought to be in a cage.'

'You mean you've been to see Doug?'

'Yes. But I didn't see him and he lives in a right dump.'

'What did you go for?' I gave myself one guess. 'Money.'

'All I want is to keep her with me.'

'You think my brother would give you money for that?'

Pike still has his own teeth and shows them in his own gums. 'I wasn't going to tell him. I was keeping her out of it. I left her in the car outside the gate. I had a story ready about you needing money and not liking to ask.' I laughed out loud then because that's all Pike knows about Doug and me – after being married to me a life-time. 'I walked up to the house and while I was gone this freak frightened the life out of her.'

'Freak?'

'She was screaming. When I ran back he had his head in the car window.'

'Freak?' I said again.

'She was hysterical. I chased him away but I couldn't calm her down. She's so highly strung; it's bad in her condition. It's bad to get worked up.'

'Don't worry about her. She's like her mother, dizzy as a gnat. Gnats don't run into big trouble.'

'It turned me up. He only had half a face. Christ knows what the other half was. He was reaching into the car to get his hands on her. I pulled him out by the scruff of his neck. He was foaming at the mouth –'

'Surely not.'

'I tell you he was like a wild animal!'

'He was frightened.'

'He was mad.' Pike blinked. 'He had flowers in his hair.'

I laughed. He picked up the bag and went to the door. I said, 'She doesn't have to have it, you know. She could get rid of it.' That was unkind, he wanted to believe the child was his, but the sooner he faced the truth the better. Everything I do for him is for the best.

He said, 'She's started buying things.'

'What things?'

'For the baby.'

'That rabbit?'

'She wants it and I want it.'

'The rabbit?'

'The baby.'

He didn't say goodbye, or what will you do. He simply went, leaving the wardrobe full of their clothes and her suitcase under the bed and his flannel on the shutter.

And that rabbit in the yard with the empties. If it had been to hand I'd have torn the stuffing out. Toys like that are dangerous for young babies.

I don't bear malice. If Cherrimay gives birth, good luck to her. And to Darlene. Darlene will need luck, she'll be a grandmother once removed. Removed from the father who is not her son-in-law and in all probability a total stranger and in all probability no

88

more than a random guess for Cherrimay. He certainly isn't my husband.

I waited to see if Pike would come back for the rest of their things, but he didn't: Cherrimay, weeping her head off, wouldn't notice that they were short of luggage.

He was right about one thing: I need not stay. I hated the place, I couldn't wait to get away. I packed my bag and took it to the hall. Madame Rosy came out from under the tapestry. She handed me two bills, one for more than twice the other.

'What's this?'

'It is the account of Monsieur and Madame Pew.'

'And?'

'Monsieur Pew has said you will pay.'

'Has he indeed.' I counted out four hundred-franc notes. 'This is for my room, a lot more than it's worth, and all you're getting.'

'There is again a thousand francs, Madame.'

'That's nothing to do with me.'

'You have said he is your husband.'

'My husband's name is Pike.'

For a moment she was all green for go. 'In France we call such a fish "un brochet".'

I screwed up their bill. 'You may keep what they've left in lieu.'

'Madame?'

'I'm not paying.'

'It is the law.'

'I'm not liable for what they owe. Any lawyer, even a French one, will tell you that.'

'It is unfortunate –'

'Not for me.'

'I regret, if you do not pay you cannot leave.'

'Try and stop me.'

I turned. There was a man in the doorway, a big man, black as coal, grinning like a piano.

I had yet to see an expression on Madame Rosy's face; the paint was too thick to let anything through. Though I could make a guess. She was probably looking triumphant. 'I shall report this to the British Consul.'

She smoothed out Pike's bill. Her nails were green like her eyelids, the untreated skin on the backs of her hands bluish and scaly. No wonder, she'd blocked up her pore-holes.

I paid. It was worth it to get out of that place. The negro showed all his white notes when he let me pass.

Pike had shown initiative. He must have been desperate – for Cherrimay Pugh, the mother of his child. I can't respect a fool or his folly, but I had to respect its origin. Pike has the makings of a man but not the mix. I respect his ambition, it's the same as mine for him: I've fostered and tried to further it. Without success. Here was Cherrimay Pugh, with no trouble at all, with probably the greatest pleasure, demonstrating that someone had been a fully paid-up man. And here was my poor Pike, ready and eager to believe he was that man. A father. Cherrimay had him in the palm of her hand. She had me in her palm too.

I sat myself down at the pavement café. The girl in the pink satin trousers and rosebud bra appeared at the entrance to the hotel. She crossed her knees and folded her arms to make a display shelf for her breasts, and leaned her shoulder on the doorjamb, not filling the doorway like the negro, but decorating it. She drew the eye, she drew mine, and I was getting the old gynaecological pain. Two men crossed the street, a French sailor and a hunchback. The hunchback got to her first. She put her arms round his hump and they went into the hotel.

'Madame?' said the waiter.

'Forget it.' I took up my bag and walked away.

I don't like waste. There's only so much in the world and we're getting through it, things are being finished up. Soon there won't be anything left worth having, we shall eat dirt and drink rain. Sometimes I think we're here to get rid of it all, ourselves included. It seems long-winded, but God has plenty of time. And it starts, before they get round to destroying the animals and the forests and polluting the seas, with people wasting their own resources. They do it out of ignorance, like Cherrimay.

Or for money, like that pro in the rosebud bra. At least she appreciates she's dealing in something valuable.

I stood in the street, my bag beside me. There was no sun to go down, just yellow sky and the earth-grabbers floodlit in their glass tower. I had lost track of time. It was getting late, I needed somewhere to stay overnight. I thought why not Doug's place. I hadn't yet managed to see him and it could be five more years before I got another chance.

It came to me as I stood in the grand place – quite a lot was coming to me just then – that I'd benefit from talking. Not to gripe or be comforted; to sort things out. There were things I needed to say and I needed someone to hear them. My brother was handy. He's a success, and it's true to say he's done it by wasting himself. He couldn't have got where he is if he'd tried to make the best of himself. The people he mixes with don't want his best, or anyone else's. There's no money in it.

I don't envy him, he has had to work at it. And I knew it would amuse him to hear I'd lost my husband to Darlene's little daughter, it would bring on a smile, but he's so full of himself that anything I said would go in one ear and out the other. And that's how I wanted it; I didn't want it remembered.

I turned my back on the hotel. Words can mean anything and nothing. Whose joke was it to call it the 'Grand Place'? Only a fly on the wall could have found grandeur in that place.

A taxi was putting down a fare at the corner. I asked the driver to take me to Ile-Marie. He muttered. 'Rex Snowdon,' I said. He opened his mouth and tapped a gold tooth. I got into the cab and we drove off.

When I can't sleep I think about what Pike and the girl might be doing; I run through his repertoire. There isn't much. But a child's another matter, a child is a fact, born or unborn, a fact I have to deal with because Pike thinks it's his.

'Do you take many people up there?' I asked the driver. 'To Rex Snowdon's?' He nodded. 'What sort of people?'

'Onglay, Americain, Yapponay.' He turned in his

seat, pulled his eyes into slits and grinned.

I didn't say any more, but he did. He talked all the way; he seemed to be having a row with himself and a lot of fun. He kept turning round and laughing even though there are places on that road with no more than a tin fender between the car wheels and several thousand feet of air.

He drew up with tyres spitting grit outside Doug's gate and flashed his gold tooth. 'Wulla!'

'Wait here for me.'

He put out his hand. 'Truss aunt.'

'I want you to wait.'

He licked his finger and wrote 300 in the dust on his windscreen.

'It's too much.' But I thought if Doug's not here I'll have to go back to Nice. 'I'll pay later.'

'Madame –'

'Stay!' I pointed to the ground, as if commanding a dog, and it worked. He leaned against his cab and watched me go.

Doug's garden was dead quiet. The wind had dropped. A vine thing had been torn up and lay across the path. Its fleshy flowers had died a fleshy death. The dark in the depths of the undergrowth was Brown Windsor soup colour. Soon it would be Brown Windsor everywhere. I saw no sign of life around the house. All but one of the upstairs shutters were still closed.

I thought this is the third time I've come and it's not lucky; I'm not going to find Doug. I thought there are a lot of things I'm not going to do. Suddenly I was tired, I was tired to death. It had been a long week. Only one week since Pike left home, only five days since I followed him. If there was a button I could have pushed, just switched myself off and been done with, I would have.

I went into the front porch. The bell pull was rusted solid. Something flapped down and skimmed away over my head; a bird, a bat perhaps. There was no letter box, there is a tin nailed on a post at the end of the track for his letters.

My brother was born the same as me. My father was different but Doug and I are the same – my mother's

92

flesh and blood. And she was definitely standard. If Doug's a success – I'm not referring to the films and the money he's made, but what he's got out of his life – if it's more than I've got he may have it, but how much can he take? Can he appreciate? Because it would be like him, it would be him all over, to value only what he hasn't got.

I'm single-minded and single-hearted. I chose Pike because I thought I saw everything in him I wanted. As it turned out, the every thing was missing.

Doug has tried to be different and it's cost him. He's ending up nobody, living in a nowhere place. I used to be happy being like everyone else, and in the expectation of it. That was years ago. I never wanted to be different, but I'm the one that is. I've been forced to be. That's how it's turned out.

I passed the grotto. It was dark in there, not a glimmer from the water in the stone basin where first I'd seen that face. Some things don't improve with thinking. They're unproductive, you end up with a personal minus.

I had Pike to think about, and Cherrimay: those two. Those three, if Pike is to be believed.

That's what I'm up against. He can be trusted to believe, but not to be believed. Cherrimay Pugh needn't be carrying his child, or any child. With him it's the thought that counts. There's a limit, there's nine months. Even Pike knows how long it takes to produce a child. If Cherrimay doesn't produce, he'll have to accept that he's not a father. On the other hand, if she has a child, if she has a miscarriage or even a false pregnancy, he'll be certain he's a father. A *father:*

Darlene cried all the time she was carrying. Cherrimay takes after her mother and Darlene's quite equal to crying while Cherrimay's carrying. Or not carrying. We were in for a wet winter.

At the back of the house I came upon young Jekyll and Hyde emptying the dustbins. He was tipping the rubbish into an oildrum mounted on pram wheels.

He was still wearing those baggy jeans, no shirt, no shoes. And Pike was right, there were flowers in his hair, blue funnel-shaped flowers stuck into the Afro mass. On anyone else it would have looked silly, but that's one thing his face can't look, whatever's added.

When he saw me the Hyde side had a sort of spasm; it was smiling perhaps. He left the bins and came to me. How long and clever his toes looked, he could have peeled a banana with them.

'Well, we meet again.' I felt myself colouring up. Blushing is for girls, I go dark like overdone beef. 'Where's Mr Snowdon? I'm his sister, I told you, didn't I? I'm Miss Snowdon.' Jekyll was wooden but Hyde twitched. 'I'm going home tomorrow. To England. I'm here to see my brother.'

At the same moment I was asking myself what would I do if he appeared. Doug was the last person I wanted to see. I didn't want to see anyone or have anyone see me. At that moment in time it was all then and there.

But you can't get anywhere without lies. So who was I lying to? A lie has to be understood or it's not a lie.

'Let me look at you,' I said. I had to know just what had frightened Cherrimay out of her wits. The thought did cross my mind. Suppose she gave birth to a child with a screwed-up face, what would Pike do then? But God wouldn't stoop to that.

The face was so close I could see in detail all the pinches and tucks. When a *thing* is damaged it means someone has burned or broken a finished object. With flesh and bone the damage can start in the mix. Pastry crumbles and green wood swells. There was no knowing what had happened to this boy, whether he had been dropped or scorched or badly done. His face didn't frighten, it moved and disturbed me. But then I'm older, I don't frighten easily and I'm not pregnant. That's two plusses and a minus. Things were looking up. Ever so slightly.

Jekyll didn't smile, he left that to Hyde. It was Hyde who kissed me. I'd been waiting years, donkeys' years my time – the calendar year is for calendars – and how many girls would bring themselves to be kissed by that stitched-up mouth? We sank to our knees, drew each other down. It was need, not passion.

I ask myself who makes love? Animals don't, nor do people. Love is there or it isn't. We do what we must and we're not answerable for the way we work any more than guns are for the killing they do.

We clung to each other, rolling and devouring each other. With Pike I used to keep my eyes open. I had no faith and tried to see where I wasn't going. But this boy knew what Pike had never known. He took me without by-your-leave or foreplay, he took me with him. Who said it's better to travel than to arrive – anyone half way to normal doesn't need me to tell them it's all marvellous.

His power and mine – that's how the world was made. And I was one of the last to know it. I had my eyes shut because I knew where I was going and I knew I'd get there. I cried aloud things that I'm glad I can't now remember. If I'm required to rise above myself in future I shall need help. I was fully conscious that I'd never get another moment of glory like this one. No need to remind myself to make the most of it: you don't quantify at a time like that.

It ended in comic strip. Naturally – some of Pike's nature has rubbed off on me. And naturally I wasn't aware what else in the wide world might be happening. There was no world, just the wide, wide me. When I looked up into black beady eyes it seemed like snakes hanging over me.

Then I saw it was a flock of Christmas dinners. Surrounding us, swaying their big soft bosoms and snapping with their big hard beaks. Aiming at my face, trying to peck out my eyes. I rolled away. They came after me, trod on me with their big hard feet.

They say a swan can break a man's arm. These birds pulled my hair and nipped my behind. I expected to be pecked to death and wondered how long it would take them to do it. One stood on my back and beat its wings and they all stretched their necks and honked. It sounded like dirty laughter.

Then they went quiet, as if they'd been called off. The bird on my back trod through my hair. I heard rustling and subdued cackling. They were moving away.

The white birds going leisurely through the grass and him following was the last I saw of the boy. A picture remembered from a book of fairy stories. And now that there was nothing to smile at or delight in, it was real.

3

Bysshe had been looking forward to going home with all strings detached. He might have known he wouldn't get away so easily. A publicity sendoff, war dances on the runway and an elephant parade through the departure lounge would have been enough for Erckmann. A private departure, one man going back to his own place, was too much. Erckmann could die of quiet: it was the death he was fighting off.

Bysshe flew from Brazzaville in the company of Hilda Latouche and Nat Twoomey. Hilda was the journalist, Twoomey the photographer commissioned to do a feature on Rex Snowdon, newly retrieved for Erckmann's classic about the life of Anatole Zwemmer. The casting had been a long throw – Erckmann liked it to be known as his stroke of genius.

Certainly it had taken supersensibility to visualize Rex Snowdon in the part. Erckmann had said more than once that Snowdon was unaware of his potential, didn't know he had it in him. Erckmann had said it before invited and uninvited audiences, cuddling up to Bysshe from his four feet ten inches, the inference being that Snowdon was Erckmann's Pandora's box and what was allowed out was at Erckmann's artistic discretion.

Bysshe's conception of the part had been fundamental. He saw Zwemmer as a man moved by hate and paranormal disgust, for whom the only answer was to rub his own nose in the world's dirt. It had activated the actor in Bysshe and he had kept it private. Erckmann hadn't suspected.

Erckmann had been prodigal of Zwemmer's amoralities. 'This guy's been a baddie all his life, searching for his real self. That's part of it. He doesn't realize he's got to *lose* himself, be purified by suffering. Okay, so it's other people's suffering – that's where he loses himself. But he's a full man first, a sinner: that's how you get to be a saint.' When Bysshe suggested that some people were born good, Erckmann waved a dismissive hand. 'They're no help to the rest of us.'

Bysshe let Erckmann think he was portraying Zwemmer as a man beset by splendid demons, arcane horrors and superpowers. It was Erckmann's own cherished conception – one of the easiest to realize. Bysshe had played along with it, given a deeply focused performance of a 'haunted soul, a condemned heart'. Those were Erckmann's own words, believing, as he did, that the pure in heart must by definition be heartless.

Erckmann was a romantic and what could be more romantic than having a latter-day saint played by a current sinner. Now he was looking for a personal story to titillate the popular imagination. Something moody and magnificent, high-class erotica. And all Bysshe could hope to supply were the usual dreary little transgressions which no longer shocked anyone. He felt himself to be in a tight scenario, he who longed for freedom of action and – preferably – inaction.

He was glad to be leaving Africa: it would never be his place. The lack of discrimination offended him. The ants couldn't wait for carcasses, they fed on living flesh: frogs snapped up the ants and great birds stalked about spiking up the frogs as if they were wastepaper. The jungle was a digestive tract, and the spirit of Africa was appetite. Dissolution and decay consoled him: this system of eat and be eaten turned his stomach.

He was looking forward to getting home. But not with Latouche and Twoomey. They were sure to produce some lucid shots of Ile-Marie and a grainy reputation for him. No one wanted truth from Hilda. She specialized in the sort of scurrilo-moral essay that was most sought after and enjoyed. Rumour had it that some people paid her to do a job on them.

She was talking to Twoomey. Seated across the gangway, they had their heads together, Twoomey's still under the bushwhacker's hat which he had worn in Africa. Hilda used her hands when she talked, carrying on a double entendre, unsaying what she was saying as much as implementing it. You could be in several minds with Hilda, none of them hers. When she caught Bysshe's eye she lifted her sunglasses for a steady appraisal – unwarranted because she had had plenty of chance to do that in Africa.

Twoomey also looked at Bysshe, tilting back his hat with a howdy-pardner gesture. Erckmann had brought them out on location to do the story on Zwemmer-Snowdon but they hadn't come up with anything to please him and he had told them: 'Go back to his place, wherever that is, and pull out the plug.' Useless for Bysshe to protest that surely Hilda could write as well in Africa as in France. If not better. Erckmann had turned on him: 'You were the housewives' choice in the days when there were housewives and it's going to take art to update you. I picked you for Zwemmer and people said to me, "Snowdon makes movies?" and I said, "Not that one. This is the Snowdon you saw in *Dreams Are Not Enough,* and *Wuthering Heights*. It's Rex like in Oedipus."' 'I was never in *Wuthering Heights* –' 'Isn't that what I'm saying? Believe you me, nobody will forget you were in *my* picture.' Erckmann, who was as uninhibited as he was small, had climbed on a table which was big and laid for lunch and postured among the vichyssoise. 'It's a classic. Twenty years from now they'll still be talking about Erckmann's Zwemmer.'

Africa, from this height, was a dish of cooked spinach. People down there were cooked too, half-digested and still clinging to a separate existence: the whites soft-boiled, the blacks glossy with gastric juices. There was another extreme, people picked to the bone and rocks bitten into dust.

Would he like a drink, asked the air hostess with rare

percipience. Bysshe ordered a daiquiri. Hilda hauled herself across the gangway. Unfortunately there was a spare seat next to him.

'Prophylactic.' She filled a paper cup from a vodka bottle.

'Against what?'

'Erckmann's phoney pustules. I find them more contagious than the real thing. Why didn't he bring in local talent instead of lot hoppers?'

'Perhaps because the real thing doesn't look real on the screen.'

'Do you ever wonder what sort of business you're in?'

The plane started bucking, and there was a noise from the luggage area as if a pride of lions was breaking out. Bysshe said, 'It's an air current. We experienced turbulence at this altitude when we flew in.'

Hilda drained her cup. 'When you've seen their roads you don't expect them to fill in their air pockets.'

'I expect to die each time we hit a bump.'

'Is that why you hold on to the whiskers?'

'Why should it be why?'

'To cover up your air panic. And then there's the rest.'

'What rest?'

'Broken veins, dewlaps, superannuation. I wish I could get behind something. I'd grow a beard and moustaches like a Norseman.'

'I hadn't thought about it.'

'You're lucky. Women have to put on faces in the morning and take them off at night. It's time-consuming.' Hilda spilled vodka over them both as she refilled her cup. 'How do you see yourself?'

'Much better for getting this part.'

'It gave you the chance to act and you're still at it. You know that? I've watched you keeping up the routines, stroking your beard like it's a nice cat, flexing your nostrils, walking stiff-legged, and last night you did that shot where he empties his whisky into the river all over again.'

'In my case it was beer and there was a fly in it.'

'You know what I think, I think actors never give up a

100

part. They keep it by and keep trying it for size. I don't trust actors.'

Being herself devious, there was small chance she would write anything acceptable. Acceptability was a question of taste, and on this occasion the taste had to be Erckmann's, Erckmann who was fond of saying that qualitatively speaking, all publicity was good.

When they put down at Nice, Hilda's vodka bottle was tucked into the seat-net while her upturned palms cradled an empty paper cup.

Twoomey said, 'This is the only time she gets rest, when she's travelling.'

'She's out cold.'

'She says she never found any benefit from being unconscious. If she's on the move and she's getting somewhere in time and space she feels vindicated and she can sleep.'

Bysshe took the cup. Empty-handed, she looked pathetic, as if she was asking for alms. 'We'll have to carry her.'

'I've got to carry my cameras.'

'You take her feet.'

'She's a very sensitive lady.'

'Take her torso if you think that would make her feel better.'

'Hilda hates to miss anything. If it's happening, she's got to know, and what she don't know hasn't happened.'

With difficulty they steered her into the gangway. One of her arms dropped between Bysshe's legs and caused him further difficulty. He got Twoomey to support her while he lifted the arm and positioned it across her chest. As soon as they started moving her again the arm slid off her chest. There was inevitability about the way it dropped straight into Bysshe's crotch, partly due to the law of gravity but more especially, he couldn't help feeling, to Hilda herself.

Once off the plane he fetched a luggage trolley and they sat her on it. Twoomey snapped Bysshe trundling her over the tarmac. 'A vignette. Might be useful.'

'As blackmail?'

101

'Not of Hildy. She'd only pay up if she was whitemailed.'

'Me?'

'I should hope you've got something better to hide.'

Between them they manhandled Hilda into a cab. Twoomey refused to be parted from his cameras and rode with them on his knees. The road to Ile-Marie was steep and every time it looped Hilda toppled out of her corner. She would certainly have dealt herself a straight uppercut on the front seat if Bysshe hadn't pushed her back. She came forward slowly, eyes closed, dreamily smiling, and he had the absurd impression that he was preventing her from some act of tenderness.

Ile-Marie being in the change and decay business, he never knew how far it might have progressed when he returned after absence. During the weeks he had been away something terminal might have happened, like the roof falling in. Then the two kinds of comfort, body's and soul's, would conflict.

As the taxi wallowed along the track a raucous honking followed them.

'What's that?'

'Geese.'

'This a farm?'

'I keep them as watchdogs.'

'Why not have dogs?'

'Geese are less trouble. They keep the weeds down. I give them mashed potato and cereal and a few old greens and they give me eggs.'

'They sound ugly.'

'No, they're pretty placid. The Greeks and Romans used them as sentries.'

'What are you afraid of?'

'Barbarians.'

There were scratches in the dust where Gluvas had switched it with the bunch of gorse he used as a broom. That, and opening the shutters were the sole acknowledgements of Bysshe's homecoming.

'This it?' said Twoomey.

'Welcome to Ile-Marie. I've mislaid my key. Again. Someone said routine makes a home.'

Twoomey got out of the car. He formed a frame with his hands and looked through at the house. 'It's lovely. Gone Without the Wind.'

'I'll go round the back and open up. Try and wake Hilda.'

He was glad to see that the bins had been emptied. And yes, Madame Gluvas had cleaned the kitchen. Her presence was still palpable. She and Gluvas lived on onions and she sweated them. There was a baguette on the table with ants trekking its length. They were few, and seemed to have no actual concern with the bread. Unlike the traveller ants he had seen killing chickens in Africa only days before.

He brushed the insects away and put the loaf on the dresser. In the hall he trod on grit which had blown in under the door. Obviously there had been a mistral.

Twoomey was unloading the luggage while the cabdriver talked to Hilda. 'Tell him to can it,' said Twoomey, 'she can't hear a word.'

The driver slapped Hilda's face. Bysshe said, 'I think he thinks we've drugged her in order to have our evil way with her body.'

'Tell him who you are.'

'He knows who I am.'

'Then tell him who she is.'

They got rid of the driver by opening Hilda's flight-bag and demonstrating her reserve of two bottles of vodka wrapped in her nightdress. He went away tipping his hand to his mouth.

'What's this place called?'

'Ile-Marie. Don't ask why it isn't an island.'

'I guess you don't need water to cut yourself off.'

'Help me get her inside.' Hilda was starting to snore.

'This is your island.'

'It's where I choose to live.'

'In the boondocks.' Twoomey looked bright. 'I'll get hold of shots of those panic scenes from your premieres – when women used to pull your hair out – and line them with a king-size view of here. Caption: "Where he goes to escape the barbarians."'

'Take her feet.' Bysshe propped Hilda's bag on her chest and they carried her with some difficulty up to a room on the first floor. 'I'll put you next door in case she needs anything in the night.'

'I can't supply what she needs in the night.'

They laid her on the bed and Bysshe took her shoes off. As he covered her with a blanket she reached up and hung her arms round his neck.

'Looks like you can,' said Twoomey, walking out.

Hilda pulled Bysshe down and nuzzled his beard. 'Stay with me.'

There followed a struggle to get him on to the bed. He jackknifed, held himself off at arms length, both hands braced on the pillow. He was aware that his back must be arching like a randy tom's.

Hilda was not physically undesirable, but just now he wasn't in the mood to make fond, or unfond, love. And if he were to, he knew that all his private inclinations would be immortalized in print. On the other hand, he had better not seem to be rejecting her.

He allowed himself to be drawn to sitting position on the edge of the bed and then, bringing into play the element of wonder requisite for a first caress, put a strand of hair back from her face. 'You're tired.' He gently broke her hands from his collarbone and brushed each palm with his lips. 'Try and get some rest.'

'Snowdon, you just spoke one of the two corniest bits of dialogue in films. I'll tell you what the other one is tomorrow.' Hilda opened an eye and stared. The effect was of a prolonged wink.

Bysshe told Twoomey he hoped he liked spaghetti. 'I could supplement with eggs.'

'I'd prefer steak and a beer.'

'I can manage the beer, but tinned spaghetti is all I've got in the house.'

Twoomey sighed. 'What's your set-up?'

'As you see, I'm alone.'

'You've had women.'

'None of them home-lovers. I have an old fellow who sees to the garden and his wife cleans up in the house.'

'There's no one else?'

'A boy who takes care of the geese.'

'If I make money, I spend it, and if I don't make money I spend it. You make more in a week than I do in months, so what do you do with it?'

'Bury it. Like the peasants.'

'What a way to live.'

'I've come to it by a process of elimination. I've tried country mansions, penthouse suites, hotel apartments, a hunting-box in Brooklyn, Dracula's castle in Beverley Hills, a houseboat on the Seine and a yacht on the Med. I'm suited here.'

Twoomey flipped his braces and Bysshe, who at times questioned his own contentment, guessed that Twoomey was looking for a reason. Bysshe had one worked out, tracing back to the moment of his conception, when an arbitrary shower of genes and globins had given him blatant good looks and a retiring disposition. Being on permanent display and not having it in his nature to display himself, he had compromised by displaying other people. That was how he made his living. He might say he made one living in order to provide for another, quite different one. But he saw no reason to explain that to Twoomey.

'Hilda will like it.'

'I wouldn't have thought she appreciated the simple life.'

'We thought you'd live in a reconstituted barn with a jacuzzi.'

'She must have been talking to my agent.'

'She doesn't talk to agents.' Twoomey came to the stove to watch the spaghetti being stirred into a pan. 'In Africa I got steak, elephant and antelope. I fly to Europe and get a can of worms.'

'I'm sorry. I haven't had time to fetch supplies. I could make you an omelette.'

'Hilda likes to do her own groundwork.' Hilda, too, would look for a reason. She would come up with dope or gambling or alimony or deviationism. 'Hildy's the artist. I'm the camera. The lens is in my head and the picture's in my mind. Maybe it's one you'll never see, but it's there. I take it with my eyes – the light, focus, composition, texture, I'm one hundred per cent in control, no silicon chip's going to do my job for me.'

'Have you any idea what Erckmann wants?'

'My business is to show the world the inner man. It'll be up to Hilda to make that right with Erckmann.'

'Which means she'll make me a good old-fashioned muckrake.'

'She'll do what's best for all of us. She wanted this job and she went out of her way to get it.'

'I thought it was Erckmann who wanted her.'

'He did, once he knew she was interested. What's that you're putting in?'

'Plonk du Place. To stimulate the tomato sauce. Would you say it's a good or a bad thing, her being interested? For me, I mean, in the final analysis?'

'It's a waste of time speculating. How you come out will depend on factors. Hers.'

Bysshe had been to the village and back before Hilda emerged next morning. She moved as if she was stuck down with Sellotape. But as her drunkenness had seemed more a ploy than a frailty, he was cheered that she actually had a hangover. She looked dewy but unfresh.

She came into the kitchen as he was unpacking the shopping. A rare steak lay bleeding on the table. Hilda took one look and walked out.

Bysshe called 'Sorry!', pushed the meat into the fridge and swabbed the table. Hilda came back. 'Twoomey fancies steak. I had to disappoint him last night, he only got tinned spaghetti.'

'Where is he?'

'I don't know. He went out before I did.'

On Hilda make-up was a concession: without powder, lipstick and the burned-blanket tint she used on her eyelids her face gave no quarter. Bysshe poured coffee, black and strong, expecting she would be glad of it. She took it to the sink and poured it away. 'Is the water potable?' Bysshe nodded. She filled the cup and drank. 'I couldn't find the bathroom.'

106

'What?'

'In the middle of the night I needed to evacuate. I couldn't find where to do it.'

'From your room it's up one flight of stairs and halfway up another.'

'You left me in ignorance.'

'I left you sound asleep.'

'I ended up on a balcony which was lucky. I managed, but it's not an experience to be enshrined in the memory.'

'I'm sorry.'

'Show me the house.'

'Of course –'

'Not now, for God's sake. Before nightfall is all I ask, before dark. What's with your dark? It's blacker than Africa. When I did finally find a switch and pressed, nothing happened.'

'The bulb must have blown. I'll see to it.'

'What's that smell?'

'You mean this?' He peeled *Nice-Matin* from a sizeable fish. 'It's for supper.'

Hilda lowered herself into a chair, she was plainly at risk up to, but not including, her eyeballs. There was nothing vulnerable about them. 'I don't eat catfish.'

'This isn't catfish. See, it's got quite a big mouth. Perhaps it's a pike.'

He hadn't thought of Dulcie in months. She rarely surfaced and when she did it was usually, as now, at the bidding of his jokey subconscious. He could guess what Hilda would make of Dulcie, and of Pike. Dulcie Bysshe married a fish. It wasn't safe to think about her in Hilda's presence.

'Tell me about the house.'

'I bought it before prices rocketed, the house and several acres of land – garden, orchard, meadow and a stand of Kermes oaks. It had been a family apportionment, passing to the next in line without anyone actually living in it or looking at it. It came on the market when the last of the family died. I saw it from the air.'

'You saw it and fell in love with it.'

'Hardly. It looked like a collar stud on a cabbage leaf.

But I did think, now that would be a secluded spot.'

'Is it?'

'People tend to find their way here.'

'People you don't want?'

'People I could do without.'

'Women?'

'It's ungracious of me.'

'Yes.'

Bysshe, who had been fifty per cent sincere, wondered at the tartness of her tone. He put it down to hangover which, as he knew from experience, is better one minute and infinitely worse the next. 'I shouldn't object to my audience seeking me out. But when they come and stare as if I'm a bad accident –' He observed that Hilda was not staring at him or anything else, she was fighting it out with the daylight. 'Could I get you something? Seltzer? Aspirin?'

'Nothing.'

The fish bothered him. He carried it to the sink. Through the window he saw Twoomey coming across the yard. Twoomey held his hat in the crook of his arm, his camera cradled on it. Bysshe cut off the fish's head. 'Excuse me.' He spoke to Pike rather than the fish. He had always felt sympathy for Pike.

Twoomey sent the door crashing against the wall when he came in.

'Damn you!' cried Hilda.

'Sorry, Hil. You should have been with me. I've been looking round. There are big clouds with plenty of depth and I hate to waste depth. Is there breakfast?' Bysshe poured him a cup of coffee. 'Ham and eggs?'

'Sorry. There are croissants.'

'I asked myself what would Peter Paul Rubens have done with these clouds. If he could have been here with a Polaroid, in his own time, never having seen a jet or a TV show, what sort of picture would he take. The answer was my sort. P. P. Rubens, being a great artist, he'd have had no choice.'

Hilda said, 'A commercial photographer has no business being modest.'

Twoomey dunked a croissant. 'I'd reached that

108

conclusion when I turned around and saw something P. P. Rubens never did. Well, to the best of my knowledge and belief he's left no record of it.' He carried the croissant, dripping, to his mouth. 'You might have warned me.'

'You got a surprise?' said Bysshe.

'I would, wouldn't I?'

'He's harmless.'

'Who is?' said Hilda.

'A kid with half a face. Split down the middle. One side's good-looking, the other's a disaster.'

'A kid?'

'How did he get that way?'

'I don't know,' said Bysshe.

'Someone surely screwed him up.'

Hilda was taking notice. Those fine nostrils of hers were picking up a scent.

'I know nothing about him. He turned up here a year or so ago. He comes and goes as it suits him. When he's here I give him food and a few francs for helping about the place. He sleeps in Gluvas's fort.'

'Where?'

'A shed in the orchard.'

'What's his name?'

'I don't know. He doesn't talk. He can't, he's almost completely deaf. To me he's the oieboy.'

'The what?'

'"Oie" is French for goose.'

Hilda closed her eyes. 'If I remember rightly there was a goose*girl*. In the fairy tale. She was a ninny but she had a talking horse. What's this gooseboy got?'

'Zilch.'

'He's happy enough,' said Bysshe.

'Enough for him, you mean?' Twoomey mopped into his coffee cup with another croissant. 'That don't amount to much.'

'What was he doing?'

'Sitting in a pool with his knees to his chin, splashing. Seeing all that frizzy hair I thought he was a girl. Venus observed, I thought, I'm in luck. Then he looked round.'

'There's a pool?' said Hilda.

'It surfaces in a shallow cave in the rock,' said Bysshe. 'A small pool fed by an underground spring. He uses it as a bathroom.'

Hilda stood up. 'Where?'

Bysshe said, 'There's one at the end of the passage.'

Twoomey said, 'Across the yard, left at the prickly pear and down the track. But the kid's gone. He took off when he saw me. Mother-naked. P. P. Rubens would have liked it.'

They watched Hilda cross the yard, perching on her hipbones. 'Trying to break the Sellotape,' said Bysshe.

'Say?'

'The way she's walking. She looks tied up.'

'She's dedicated. Say, that kid of yours –'

'He's a migrant, with his own seasons.'

'I must get some shots of him.'

'Why?'

'Photomontage.'

'He's easily upset.'

'I won't be using a black cloth and touch powder.'

'You want to take close-ups for people to gloat over? He's not a freakshow.'

'Every picture should tell a story. There are messages everywhere and my business is to pick them up.'

'What will this message be?'

'I don't know yet. I make images to show other people. And myself. To educate myself, get into perspective.'

'How do you know you've got the message right?'

Twoomey tipped back his chair and hung his thumbs in his braces so that Bysshe felt the weight of what was coming.

'I'm surrounded by the raw material of consciousness. We all are. And what do we do? We each try to get a lion's share. But we have to relate to it and some of us don't ever get that far. The raw material of consciousness is my subject.' Twoomey tapped his forehead. 'Here's the camera and maybe I'll pick the wrong thing to show or the wrong way to show it or the wrong person to show it to. Or all three. It's still my way. I am what I am. What I'm not, is the angel with the flaming sword. I'm here to make people look.'

110

Bysshe looked, and glimpsed the fish's golden eye staring up from the sink. He wrapped the head in newspaper and took it outside.

The air was heavy with the smell of thyme, mint, rosemary, terebinth. He had once tracked each smell obsessively, gone about his garden on all fours, sniffing like a dog. Now there was the fish smell. He threw the parcel into a bin, knowing that he might well have bought a lobster for his supper if he had been alone. But the smell of fishy newspaper was evidence that he was not alone. As if he was in need of conviction, as if he was liable to forget there were foreign bodies present, as if his hackles weren't stirring –

Bysshe rammed the lid on the bin and walked across the yard to the garden. Latouche and Twoomey, enemy aliens, posed a limited threat. They would interrupt his way of life, interpret the interruption, and leave. He picked up a carob pod and cracked it. He didn't fancy their chances here, any more than he fancied his own. He was glad about his own, however, and breathed in the sweet smell of decay.

He had a mind to see Gluvas. Gluvas was a creature of the place, had lived here all his life and was openly sceptical of the existence of anything beyond the Estoril. If Ile-Marie wanted a voice, it had to be his – the old devil without a drop of charity in him. Ile-Marie's strength and saving grace was its inhumanity. It was proof that one could be freed of all responsibility – moral, social and personal – and look forward to desiccation, to the ultimate conclusion; a little calcium dust on carbonated beetle wings.

But it was Bysshe who wanted a voice. Somehow he couldn't feel that he had been received back until he had heard Gluvas, he needed to be told he was there. He went down through the orchard to the old man's 'fort', where he kept his onions and his cider. The cider was primal stuff, even Gluvas wasn't equal to more than a quart at a time and frequently slept where he dropped, among his casks.

The boy was there, alone, and motionless, though without tranquillity. He had only just stopped, the air was still spinning round him. When alarmed, he froze on

111

the brink of his next move, whether it was flight, or fight, or his brand of rejoicing.

Bysshe realized that Zwemmer's whiskers would have altered his appearance. He touched the boy on his shoulder, in reassurance and greeting. 'It's me.' The eye did not flicker: the hole in the cheek stretched, painfully.

'How have you been?' Bysshe struck a match to light a cigarillo. The boy uttered a strangled sound as the flame approached Bysshe's beard. Fire was what he feared most. Understandably. 'It's all right. Let's talk.'

Bysshe sat on a cider cask and the boy touched his own chin as if there might be tender stubble somewhere.

'Where's the old man? Sleeping it off with Madame G.? He hasn't done much while I've been away, though I can see the mistral's been busy.' Bysshe shrugged. 'At least I'm keeping the status quo going. Underdevelopment has to be paid for.'

The boy sank to his knees in a movement which a ballet dancer might envy. He sat on his heels, his bad side turned to Bysshe, who had observed that he seemed to experience, to register, on that side.

'Of course the status quo will keep going without me. The polymers and nuclear waste will start something special in due time. I'm doing this for *my* sake, so I can watch it happening. You see, I like the way recycling's done here. Discreetly. I'm just back from Africa where it's shoved under your nose. Messy. Even the trees bleed. But would you believe it – all that real life wasn't real enough for the cameras. They had to fake it.' Bysshe squared his hands and held them in front of his face to peer through them as Twoomey had done. 'And something happened to me.' He flung wide his hands. 'I was shot to pieces. And when the pieces reassembled, they weren't all mine.'

The boy gripped his own forearms. It was a movement expressive of something, and to Bysshe it seemed relevant. 'Some were Zwemmer's pieces. They must have been, how else could I have come by them. That man was a mess. I played him as a psychopath. I did heart-warming scenes when he stuck his needle into sweet old lepers and carried leper babies in his bosom.

When I raised up a dying woman I held her stumps in my hands as if they were ladies' fingers. But it wasn't tenderness, it was disgust. That was the only way I could do it, reacting in a real way to total unreality. They brought a live leper on the set, he was what's called a "burnt-out case", and from him the make-up department contrived dozens of combustibles. Variations on the theme. I ask myself how would I have felt if it was pus I was swabbing and not Vaseline jelly. Suppose they'd been live and dying people, would I have hated them? Did Zwemmer? It doesn't matter about him, he's past and done with, it's not even history, because no one will ever know what he felt. But it matters about me. I could so easily say I was disgusted because it was faked. That would be a good reason, humanly speaking. But was I? Or was I thinking into the part? Thinking myself into the part, reacting as *I* would to real disease? To do a thing for the right reason makes it all right. Are we sure about that? If we do a right thing for the wrong reason does that make it all wrong, or half right? What we're getting to is, it's not what we do that matters, but why we do it.'

One of Gluvas's onions dropped one of its skins. A fragment floated onto the boy's shoulder. He snarled like a puppy and beat it off.

Bysshe said, 'Did you do that because you don't like onions? If that's your reason, it's right. And if you dislike onions so much you shouldn't have to sleep with them. I think Zwemmer so disliked the world he gave his only beloved self in atonement.' Bysshe blew a smoke ring, the boy put a finger through it. 'I think he was bored being a rakehelly and decided to try goodness for a change because it was all that was left for him to try. And he found that even more boring. I tried to put his boredom across by shutting my eyes very slowly and opening them fast. Erckmann thought I was expressing emotion.' Bysshe blew another ring for the boy. 'I think I'm becoming addicted to these weeds. Zwemmer smoked them all the time, many a shower of ash went into the sterile dressings.'

The boy reached up to touch Bysshe's beard. His

fingers stroked it with a gentle, lingering movement. His chest swelled to a sigh. Of relief, or pleasure, or envy.

Bysshe guessed how it must look to Hilda, arriving at the shed door at that particular moment. The boy on his knees, stroking Bysshe's face, was an interesting little cameo which she might make of what she liked. And he knew the sort of thing she liked.

To do her justice, she didn't exclaim when the boy turned his face towards her. She quizzed him as she might any personable male. Her eyebrows went up slowly, she smiled a buttoned-down smile.

The boy clasped his arms across his chest. He leaped up, and flattening himself to avoid touching her, he ran from the shed.

'Strangers alarm him,' said Bysshe.

'Is he yours?' She was looking around, at the dirt floor, the onions, the stretcher-bed trampled like a dog's, cider casks, goose droppings, feathers impaled and lightly stirring on the splintered walls. Bysshe knew what she was doing: she was isolating what she could use for the story.

He said, 'So you noticed the likeness. Mind you, I don't know who the mother was. I surmise it must have been one of the village girls. I was terribly young at the time – just thirty-five – and libidinous. But it could have been any of the starlets who were around then. They used to flock to this place like moths to a candle.'

'What do you mean, you don't know who the mother was?'

'The child was left on my doorstep, in an onion bag. That made me wonder about Madame Gluvas, the gardener's wife. She was around too.'

'What does he do?'

'Comes and goes. Of his own free will.'

'Goes where?'

'I don't know. I don't ask because he can't hear me; and even if he could, he couldn't answer.'

Hilda lowered herself gingerly on to the boy's bed. She still looked groggy. 'Free will exists only in the very first years of life, at a time when we're incapable of doing anything with it. Thereafter the system is formed and

114

the IQ fixed. What's his mental age?'

'As old as the rocks I should think. Do you like herbs?'

'Why?'

'I'm considering how to cook the fish for supper.'

'I'm trying to figure what advantage a retardate of sixteen with a mental age of six would have over the rest of us.'

Bysshe had found comfort from fingering his whiskers at uncertain moments. He would miss them. He thought perhaps he wouldn't shave.

'Bollocks to supper,' said Hilda.

By evening she was taking a stimulant, white wine laced with Greek brandy. Bysshe put out chairs on the terrasse. 'You needn't worry about the bats, they won't fly into your hair.'

'I never thought they would. It's the smell that gets to me. Like supermart scent. Do they spray the grapes with it?'

'There are no grapes.'

'Then it's a herbicide, and from the look of the vegetation it's a killer.'

'Indoors smells different,' Twoomey said. 'Like there are things living in that ought to be out.'

'It's early for the rats,' said Bysshe. 'We're usually free of those until the colder weather. The mice are always with us.'

'Not to mention the bugs.' Hilda said irritably, 'You could provide nets.'

'I keep forgetting. The mosquitoes don't come after me, I've been here too long. They prefer new blood.'

'What's that noise?'

'The frogs down by the cistern. I like to hear them. They're my lullaby.'

'The kid –' said Twoomey – 'what do you call him – Warboy?'

'Pronounced as in "oiseau".'

'What's he do evenings? Go dancing?'

'With the geese.'

'Has he got a girl?'

'I shouldn't think so.'

'Why not? He's got pazazz and he's young. Young beats everything, even a face like his. I'd like to do something for him.'

'Like what?'

'Nat,' said Hilda, 'you're here as a photographer, not a plastic surgeon.'

Twoomey ran his thumb round the rim of his beercan. 'I'll take his picture – make his portrait.'

'No,' said Bysshe.

'Gotta reason?'

'I told you my reason.'

'I told you mine.'

Bysshe smiled. 'I remember. The raw material of consciousness. "I am a camera".'

'It's my work ethic.' There was entrenchment behind Twoomey's grin. 'I read it in a book and if it was good enough for Höpker and Glinn, it's good enough for me. There's no copyright in principles, and the way I look at it, I'm in every portrait I do. Because that's the way I look at it.'

'Every picture an ego trip,' said Hilda.

'I'll photograph the kid as he looks to me, as he *is* to me.'

'And people will see what you saw and make something else of it.' Bysshe knew he was stating a truism which had already been broached, and would bear going into. 'Please, don't make anything of him.'

Twoomey aimed his finger. 'I'm going to make a record of that face.'

'Why?'

'Because I saw it and I've a right to everything I see. I'm a photo-journalist, I make pictures to tell how it is.'

'There's no way to tell how it is with him.'

'There has to be. I started in a chain-portrait studio, taking pictures at ten dollars a time. They had to be the kind of pictures people would want to frame – that was the criterion, and I didn't find it demeaning. I worked on them, and when I'd finished they looked better than life. But I always found a statement to make.'

'I read somewhere that you have a twin sister,' Hilda said to Bysshe. 'What's her name?'

'Dulcie.'

116

'Dulcie Bysshe. Have you a photograph of her?'

'No.'

'When I do a picture of someone I go for the soft centre where there's usually a leak. But if there's no break in the candy I go for the fancy wrapper and make my statement.'

'Does she look like you?'

'We're not identical.'

'Neither are the two sides of any one face. Did you ever wonder what a face is? Where the original design comes from? The practical considerations aren't all that good. We'd do better with recessed holes and dermal scales. What interests me about this boy's, is which side registers which. Does the left register the same emotion as the right? Or does it come out sweet and sour, like a Chinese takeaway?'

'If looking at the original tells me nothing,' said Bysshe, 'neither will a photograph.'

'That's where you're wrong. I'll show you what's there when you're *not* looking.'

'In glorious Kodachrome?'

'Colour's a liberty I wouldn't take with him. I want him black and white.'

'What will you do with the pictures?'

'What does any professional do with his work? He gets the best price he can for it, taking into account the time and materials he's expended; or he gives it as a gift if there's someone he wants to give to; or he gets a Pulitzer; or he puts it in his portfolio and never shows anybody.'

Hilda said, 'Tomorrow you'll be working with me.'

'Doing what?'

'What we came for.'

'I forget what that is.'

She said to Bysshe, 'Shave off the lace so we can see Rex Snowdon.'

'Aren't I recognizable?'

'As a prairie dog.'

Bysshe had been surprised and charmed by the softness and luxuriance of his facial hair. When he held it, it felt like a bird in the hand. 'I was planning to keep the beard.'

'You were planning to keep Zwemmer.'

Twoomey said, 'If the human face is a piece of plumbing, whiskers are grass in the downspout.'

Bysshe experienced the old sense of annihilation, and rage that it should be happening to him here, in his place. He wanted to tell them to go away and leave him alone. 'I think I'll take a bath. Association of ideas.'

In the bathroom mirror he came face to face with Zwemmer. As portrayed in Erckmann's life of the sinner-saint: Rex Snowdon with whiskers.

He turned the bath taps. The water rushed out like ale, frothing slightly. The bubbles raced the length of the bath and expired in tiny vortices. The water came from a mountain spring, a spell in the hot tank had not subdued it. There were even times, as now, when sundry organisms came through the taps, insects and tiny amphibians.

Try as he might, he could detect neither sin nor sanctity, no signs of inner strength or moderate zanyism in his face. Had he looked the Latin lover playing Zwemmer? If so, where was Erckmann to have allowed it? Had Erckmann even noticed? Or had he approved and fostered the image? That was possible. Erckmann was a gambler who thought God was personally directing his throws. Bysshe pulled down his eye sockets and bared his teeth.

'May we share?' He swung round. Hilda was behind him, her eyebrows hitched to a sweet reasonableness. 'I do have to have one.'

'One what?'

'Bathroom. Nat's using the upstairs as a darkroom. He's blacked out the windows and locked himself in. I've nowhere to pee.'

'This is my bathroom –'

'I don't mind waiting.' She sat herself on the edge of the bath. 'Are you going to get into this soup?'

'I was.'

'Go ahead.'

'I prefer to bath in private.'

'I want to talk.'

'Not now – not here.'

'Here and now. Nat's ears are long and I'd sooner he didn't hear what I have to say. You'd prefer it, too.'

'I want to have my bath.'

'I'll scrub your back.'

He considered what he could do. He could take his bath and ignore her – try to – or he could pull out the plug on the pretence that the water was too mucky.

'I want to talk about my sister-in-law.'

Another option was to push her into the bath. He had an acceptable vision of her rising up with her dyes running.

Hilda said sharply, 'Caresse.'

It sounded like a command and he blinked. 'I beg your pardon?'

'That was her name.'

'Caresse? Caresse Latouche?'

'Latouche is my professional name. Our family name is Nussbaum. Does that mean anything to you?'

'It could mean you changed your nationality.'

'You knew my sister-in-law.'

'I never knew any one called Caresse.'

'Carrie Nussbaum, my brother's wife. She was here with you.'

Bysshe felt he was getting into a minefield. But there could be no risk in looking pleasant. Or foolish. 'Ah. Small world.'

'She's dead.'

The tone alarmed him. The words, the meaning, were not assimilable at once. They were like a blow which he needed to know the provenance of, and the purpose – if there was one – before he could actually feel it. And then she said, smugly, 'She killed herself.'

Playing for time – time out of mind – he said, 'Are you sure?' Hilda nodded, seemed not to take offence. 'When?'

'A couple of months ago.'

'Did she – what – how did she –'

'An overdose. She was never original.'

The blow was delivered, there was now no point in defending himself, but he tried. 'I didn't know. I was in Africa. We missed a lot of the American news.'

119

'She didn't make news.'

'I had no idea.' But he had it now all right, and didn't know what to do with it. Not in Hilda's presence. 'I can't believe it. She was too – sensible.' Was 'sensible' the word? There could be two interpretations and in this connection, the connection of Carrie Nussbaum, one refuted the other.

'Carrie couldn't start anything. She picked up after other people. But it was her first time for dying.' He wondered where this was leading. Hilda said, 'If her feelings were like everybody else's, it doesn't mean they weren't new to her.'

'Of course not.' He wanted to put it aside until he was alone. 'I didn't know her well.'

'Biblically you did. You were lovers.' It was a confrontation on his own ground, at Ile-Marie. He felt Zwemmer's whiskers stiffen – the old animal reflex was still there. 'She called me long distance. She said, "He doesn't want me the way a woman wants to be wanted, he used me like a kitchamajig."'

'A what?'

'Everything a man uses a woman for.'

'She wouldn't say that.'

But Hilda would. Hilda was showing her teeth in something that was only fractionally a grin. 'She told me about you and about this place. She and I were never close, and calling me up to tell about a love affair that had folded simply wasn't like her. But she'd got to the point where she had to talk to someone. Mind you, she wasn't giving anything away. No names were mentioned, it was "He", uppercase, like in God, and this place was Heaven the way she told it.' Bysshe consoled himself that even coming in by the back door – Hilda's method of entry – she would find nothing new, nothing that hadn't been done already. He too was unoriginal. 'When she'd told me all she intended to, she hung up and fixed herself a barbitone and oxyzine cocktail.' Bysshe went cold, then hot. Then sick. The back door afforded unfair advantages but he had not yet reckoned on what might be done with them in the right hands. 'By the time they got to her it was too late for a stomach pump. I suspected

120

she was going to do something and I called my brother, he's in the wig and hairpiece business. He told me their marriage was finished and he wasn't liable for her. He said he'd been cuckolded. I said did he know the word stems from the French for cuckoo and he slammed down the phone. I called the janitor of her block. He went to her apartment with his master key, but she'd bolted the door. He told me there was nothing he could do, he wasn't allowed to interfere with tenants' private arrangements.' Hilda let out a hoot which was one part laughter. 'Afterwards I put it together: the screen-lover with his love nest on the Côte d'Azur.'

'This is no nest, it's where I live.'

'And the grotto and the garden where you played ball. She told me you played ball.'

'Boules. Everyone plays boules.'

'And there were fireworks at the village carnival which you watched in bed together.'

'There are fireworks and carnivals all over France in the summer.'

'She didn't mention the boy with half a face.'

'She would have, wouldn't she?'

'Are you saying she wasn't here?'

'He's at least as remarkable as a grotto and fireworks.'

'I suppose you were just good friends.'

'We didn't have what it takes for good friendship. We were both rather bad at it.' Bysshe knew now where the blow had come from and it wasn't a clean punch. It was a spreading clout.

'I know now that I love you' she had written, and he had put the letter down the lavatory because surely she would regret sending it. When other letters came he returned them unopened. She had to know what he felt without his telling her in so many words. How many? Thousands, and all wrong. There were no right ones for telling a thing like that. But there must be some which were better chosen than others. He had doubted his ability to choose, and Carrie's to make allowances. She was more easily hurt than anyone he had ever known which had made her tiresome to be with. At times he had felt mentally cramped, trying to avoid thoughts that would damage her. Sad she was, but independently of circumstance. Life had been charitably disposed towards her, and she knew that she had no right to sorrow. She tried to disown it, with laughter and little sallies of her spirits, spontaneous and often irrelevant. In fact it was the first thing he had noticed about her, those obligated joys. He had thought then that she had to be mildly crazy, or perhaps just taking the mickey.

They had encountered each other at the Picasso museum. She was alone, so was Bysshe. She came and stood beside him as he was looking at the cartoons. He waited for her to move away because he couldn't appreciate pictures in company. He needed a private view if he was to see anything for himself.

She said, 'They frighten me.' He nodded. She said, 'I mean – if it's that simple – after all?'

'I find them refreshing.' He had walked away.

A party of German students arrived. They laughed a lot, mocking, miffed at the drawings. They were young and did not need refreshment. Finding a seagod to himself, Bysshe realized that he was looking for fright in the single line of the drawing. Her 'after all' had been a cry more than an exclamation, referring he supposed to life in general rather than a specific hassle.

He glanced sideways to where she still stood, staring over the top of her glasses at the picture. The students approached, surrounded her. She turned, listening or speaking to them. They laughed and moved on, and she was left, a tall woman, gawky, with a misapplied air. She wasn't pointing herself in the right direction. At that moment she was aimed at a picture of a mermaid with astonished breasts rising from a sea of kisses.

Bysshe went back to her. 'I suspect it is.' When she turned to him her eyes drowned under her glasses. Then swam to within millimetres of the surface. He added, smiling, 'I certainly hope so.'

He watched her take the thought and worry about it, worrying because she hadn't had it herself. Then he walked out of the Musée and was aware of her following.

It was an afternoon of occluded light, the dregs of a

dust storm in North Africa blotted out the sun. They stood on the ramparts and she told him that she had travelled from Bakersfield, USA with an arts appreciation group and had seceded for the afternoon because the group had gone to look at cave paintings. 'It frightens me, being underground. In London we took the subway to the Tate Gallery. I went down the escalator, turned around and came straight back up.' Her laugh was reflex, a gasp without vocal backing. Bysshe looked over the parapet, there were things floating on the water which he hoped she could not see. She claimed she had no knowledge of art. 'Picasso' – she said, handing it over, making him a present of her ignorance. Perhaps she thought it was owed to the conversation she hoped they were going to have about the basic simplicity of life.

A ship was slipping out of the bay. He pointed to it, sugar-white, dissolving into and sweetening the haze.

'Yes.' She pushed her glasses into her hair, unseeing.

He was himself attracted to a linear concept of life and would have liked to believe in its comedy. But he was not prepared to proselytize. And much later, when she asked if he really thought everything was simple, he knew that she was seeking guidance, not confirmation, and at that later time he had to say no.

He left her on the ramparts at Antibes with a wave of the hand, and forgot her.

When she did return, briefly, to his mind, it was via Picasso's mermaid. That came first. He had to smile, recalling the sea of kisses, fifteen – he had counted them. Also he remembered one of the students, a butter-blonde with fiery bloom along her jaw. She belonged with the mermaid. Of the woman from Bakersfield he remembered only her eyes going down for the first, or was it the second, time.

When he thought of her now it was with a sense of having forgotten more than he remembered. Because she had been slipping away, dissolving like the ship, though without sweetness. Absenting herself. As they had both agreed.

When the letters started to come he was angry: with

her, for not keeping to their agreement, and with himself because what had meant so much to her meant so much less to him. He had thought they were escaping involvement. He had been careful, even distasteful of her, because of her vulnerability and the dangers of it. He asked nothing of her, nor she, he had hoped, of him. As he saw it, they might lightly purloin anything they needed.

Going had been her move. 'I'll go,' she had said. 'And when I get home I'll forget all this.' He had teased, 'All of it?' and she had laughed her reflex laugh. 'Memories have their place and Bakersfield's not the place.'

The day following their first encounter, a bus had drawn up outside Ile-Marie. To a burst of muzak and a voice-over, the driver got out and examined the padlock on the gate. He shook the gate, kicked it and shouted. Bysshe, in a dirty singlet and ruptured jeans, was dragging a handcart up from the orchard. The driver appealed to him. Bysshe shrugged. Dozens of pairs of sunglasses levelled through the windows of the bus. The voice-over said: 'We are now approaching one of the oldest oil-mills in the area. The olives are gathered and brought for pressing. Here you have a unique opportunity to witness a method which has remained fundamentally unchanged throughout the ages –' The driver climbed into his cab, hauled on the wheel and drove off in a burst of diesel.

Then the bus stopped again and someone else got out, a woman in a chemico-pink dress and a headscarf knotted under her chin. She waved to the bus, it moved off and she walked towards Bysshe.

Carrie Nussbaum had come to Ile-Marie. She had prevailed upon the tour operator to depart from the schedule sufficiently to show her where Rex Snowdon lived. 'I thought you might be, but I wasn't sure,' she said. 'Yesterday in Antibes you looked older.' The shocking pink dress was the colour for candy, but not for her. In it, over-pinked, she was well nigh invisible.

Bysshe pointed out, 'You've lost your bus.'

She said that the tour was going to St Paul and would pick her up on the way back. Then she waited, with an air of having done all she could. He had to ask her up to the house. With any other colour he would have felt less constrained, but the strident pink was such an affront to nature – in particular the nature of Ile-Marie – that he felt he ought not to leave her alone.

He offered her lunch. She said she couldn't put him to trouble, she was being a nuisance. Bysshe said it was no trouble, no nuisance, she was welcome to what there was. She said she always seemed to arrive at wrong moments – people's mealtimes, when they were in the bath, or having a fight, or icing a cake. Bysshe demurred, said mealtime was the right time to arrive and brought out bread, goat cheese, tomatoes and a bottle of red ordinary. She said she wasn't hungry, she would wait outside.

Bysshe went to the sink to wash his hands. When he turned round she was sitting at the table. They ate together. She had a large appetite, despite her earlier protestations. And when they had finished the bread and the cheese, Bysshe fetched a basket of Mirabelles and some cat's tongue biscuits. He made coffee and by then he would have said he knew all there was need to know about her.

It was a natural, if cruel assumption. Even thirty years ago she would not have been to his taste, she would have been blanched but impure. She was a middling, and in middle-age, as might be expected, that was manifest. And he did not question his right to expect it after a mere couple of hours' acquaintance.

She started to talk about films. The group had been told that the cinema was an art form. They had listened to a talk about sound and colour, very technical, and without a single shot of any of the stars.

'Very commendable,' said Bysshe.

'I saw you in a historical film. *The Naked Flame.*'

Bysshe closed up. 'I'll show you the garden.'

People didn't know whether they were meant to admire or commiserate about his garden. Carrie resorted to the acquisition of knowledge. 'What's that long topsy thing?'

'An agave.'

'Will it fall?'

'Eventually.'

'Are those immortelles?'

'Should they be?'

'They look as if they've been here a long time.'

In the grotto she hung over the pool, stirring it with her finger as if she felt she had to do something. She asked if it was a wishing pool.

'If you like. Yes. Anything can be anything you like.'

'I've tried that. It doesn't work.' She gasped with dismayed laughter.

'It does here.'

That seemed to throw, rather than reassure her. She looked about, mistrusting what she might make of things. She saw the piece of mirror on the ledge at the back of the grotto and turned away with a question unasked. Fortunately the oieboy was not around. She would have been mortally distressed by the sight of him and Bysshe would have found that tiresome.

They went through the orchard into the meadow. The geese followed them, cackling. 'Don't run,' said Bysshe, 'they've been encouraged to harass women.'

'They're pecking my legs –'

'Tell them shoo.'

She lifted the skirt of her dress and shook it at the birds. It was a country gesture and made a picture: Carrie shaking her pink dress at the white geese. Bysshe could never afterwards determine why it was significant, or what it signified, but it recurred at incongruous moments.

The geese sidled away, honking uproariously.

'Do you encourage them to harass women?'

'No, my gardener does. It saves him trouble when people turn up whom I haven't invited and don't care to see.' She blinked at him, a weight of water on her eyes. 'Some of the taxis make extra francs telling people I'm on view in my cage and bringing them here to feed me bananas.'

'I wasn't invited.'

'That's different. We'd already met and I'm glad to see you.'

He rarely concerned himself about the colour of his

126

lies, but at least this one was neutral. He wasn't rejoiced to see her nor was he altogether sorry. Softly, softly, in a way she had, she grew on him.

She said, 'I'd better go.'

Then would have been the time to stop it, if he had had less faith in himself and more in her. It seemed such a passing thing. 'No, you'd better stay.' But her staying did, in fact, turn out to be a whole lot worse.

They spent the afternoon picking plums. They picked too many because Bysshe found it a pleasant occupation and couldn't think what else to do, though he need not have because time, with her, was apt to slip away.

'What will you do with these?' Bysshe shrugged and she offered to make jam. He agreed, thinking it would be something to occupy her.

All he could find to cook the fruit in was a stewpan. They stoned the plums and cracked the stones. It was a messy job, but Carrie said the thing was to boil the kernels with the pulp to enhance the flavour. Bysshe had no jars to pot the stuff when it was done, so she put it into a salt-glazed crock.

'It ought to be hermetically sealed. Otherwise I'm afraid it won't keep.' Bysshe hoped it wouldn't. The burnished green and gold of the fruit had reduced to a khaki porridge. 'It will be lovely with cheese. Or for breakfast on crusty bread.' She sounded wistful.

Evening came, but the tour-bus did not return. Bysshe remarked that he wouldn't have thought there was so much to see in St Paul. He poured drinks and took them to the terrasse. She hesitated on the threshold, waiting, he supposed, to be asked to join him.

'We weren't just going to look, it was to be implemented study, we each had to make a drawing or painting of something to establish creative rapport.'

'Would you say you have colour sense?'

'I like to look at the colours in Nature.'

'Then why wear an unnatural colour?'

He had decided to be honest because kindness could implicate them. It was too soon, by about half a minute, for him to realize that honesty was not going to be the best policy with her.

She stood and drowned, went down for the third time

under the pink dress. 'I'll go.'

'Where?'

'I'll wait in the road.'

'They may not come back for you.'

'I'll get transport from the village.'

'The last bus went at five o'clock.'

'I'll walk. I've stayed too long.'

'Don't be ridiculous. Come and have your drink.' He went and put his hand under her elbow. He had the idea that touching her would bring her to the surface. It was an act of curiosity, not charity. For one who drowned so easily he thought there must also be an easy revival.

The revival wasn't easy, but it was worth watching. She looked at him without fear or favour, without emotion, recognition, or intelligence. Her slowly evolving bubble eyes were covered by a pearliness, a protective membrane, so that she appeared both blind and potent. It was like watching the evolution of a mollusc on speeded-up film. But the film was too fast. He missed the actual moment of repossession, caught a glimmer, then a gleam, then beheld the unresplendent whole of Carrie Nussbaum. Holding her own against the pink.

She offered to make supper for him. He said he would find something to cook. She cried, 'It's the least I can do!' as if she had already figured out a minimum. He was warned, but not seriously, she still seemed riddable.

'You don't have to do anything.'

'I'd like to – before I go – while I'm waiting.'

She made a potato omelette and a plate tart with stewed plum filling. He would have preferred something more substantial but she was good at pastry and it was a nice enough meal.

After they had eaten, she went to the kitchen to wash up. He watched her scraping pots and swilling dishes.

'Do you have a drying-up cloth?'

'I don't dry up. Nor does Madame Gluvas. She doesn't wash up until everything's been used. I average two plates a day and the frypan's perennial. The more you leave in it, the better. Like your plum kernels, it improves the taste.'

128

'I had to wash the pan before I could cook the omelette. I'm sorry –'

'They haven't come back for you.'

'I expect they forgot.'

'You don't expect to be remembered?'

She looked at him in alarm. 'I asked them to.'

'They're not likely to now. Not tonight.'

'Tomorrow they're going to Florence, then to Venice and Rome. It makes me sick.'

'Art appreciation?'

'No, coach travel. I have to try not to upset the others. So I pretend I have got hay fever and I'm sneezing. But they're beginning to realize I'm throwing up, and nobody likes sitting near me. So I'm going to skip Italy and stay on in Nice until it's time for the flight home.'

He could have driven her to the coast, but was finding in himself a curiously compounded inertia. There was common politeness in it, and caution, and the Christian wish to save her from drowning.

When she was done in the kitchen and had left all clean and tidy, she went and sat in the garden. He found her there, hands spasmodically stirring, like separate animals, in her lap. She herself seemed tranquil, even dreamy. The pink dress put a spat on his umbers and olive greens and lion yellows. He supposed it was her attempt at making a mark, any mark. Certainly it must mean something that she should have chosen chemico-pink to do it in.

He brought her a silk shirt and a pair of jeans. 'Put these on.'

She stood up at once, no question, no surprise, pulled off the dress and let it drop. What more he saw of her did not appeal. She was big-boned and in youth would have been raw-boned. Middle-aged, her flesh looked par-boiled. There was a disharmony about her: breasts, thighs, big soft belly and pubic cup did not make up the figure of a woman, they were just the component parts hung together. And what emerged was the vulnerability which he had identified as danger to be reckoned with. Perhaps the pink, after all, had been a declaration of strength.

She pulled on the shirt and buttoned it. She had trouble with the jeans which were too tight. 'My husband doesn't like women in trousers.'

'You'll be more comfortable. And so shall I.'

Comfort was not the word. She stood clutching the fly zip in classic Venus pose, looking like an unsuccessful drag artist.

Bysshe handed her his belt to secure the jeans. Her eyes, he now saw, were blue, still with that slight opacity as if brushed with milk. He picked up the dress. 'You'll need it to go home in.' Still pink, still crude, he put it into her hands, with the bodice still rounded to the shape of her breasts. She gazed at it as at something thrust upon her and he wondered what it reminded her of. Pretending to sneeze all the way home to Rome? Bakersfield, California? 'Stay as long as you like,' he heard himself say. If it proved to be longer than *he* liked he was confident he could handle it.

She stayed five days and did not intrude on his company or time. She took over the cooking, making the meals substantial to suit his taste. She liked to do the marketing herself and insisted on paying for it as part of her keep. Their wants were few, so he let her have her way.

She spoke no French and he was curious to know how she managed in the village where they did not take kindly to foreigners. She laughed her gasping laugh. 'I give them a hundred franc note.'

'And?'

'I take what I want and they take what they want.'

Some days he did not set eyes on her for hours. He followed his own routine, working in the garden and the orchard, grubbing about, though not so as to inhibit the business of decay. She did not arouse extremes of feeling, there was something off-putting about her. Her own diffidence, probably. All he had for her were reservations, he was halfway everything about her. But he found solace in the presence of another human being without having been aware of any need for solace.

One night she came to his bed. He was watching fireworks. Through his window he could see rockets and chandeliers and the *Nice-Matin* gas balloon. She came into his room without knocking, or if she had knocked he did not hear because of the noise of the fireworks. He looked up to see her beside his bed and his first involuntary response was 'Down, Carrie!'

'What's happening?' she said. 'What's going on?'

'The village fête.'

'I thought it was a gunfight.' She panted with laughter – a big crossbreed, eager, clumsy, chicken-hearted.

'Might it have been – in Bakersfield?'

'I wasn't to know.' She could retrieve a point, like a stick. 'I'm never to know, am I?' and bring it back and drop it at the feet of the thrower. It was a kind of begging.

'Come and watch.' He pulled her down on the bed at his side, put his arm under her neck. It was well meant. She had afforded him some objective comfort, he could do as much for her.

She sighed and snatched up the sigh in a gasp. She couldn't trust anything that came from her.

'Relax, there's nothing to worry about.' He patted her with the hand that was left over from her neck. It wasn't his fault, or design, that he chanced to touch her breast. But right away there was something for him to worry about. She came up like a marble under his fingers. 'It's the village saint's day. A girl called Marie – not *the* Virgin, though I daresay she was required to be one – prayed down a thunderball on the Saracens as they tried to sack the town.'

He withdrew his hand. Good dog, I've nothing for you. The *Nice-Matin* balloon rolled in a current of air.

'I shan't be here long enough to worry.'

So that's what she was getting at. He felt a sudden principled aversion to physical contact. God knew he hadn't been pretending anything, had not put on an act, and was incurious but genuinely sorry about her. One arm under her neck was hardly an embrace.

But it was halfway to one. And he should have given her nothing to build on: a woman, any woman, could make a palace out of a wisp of straw, and Carrie could do

131

it on less. He was afraid for her.

His arm was in the crook of her neck. He began gently to withdraw it. She turned her cheek into his hand. He thought Oh God, knowing he had only himself to blame. It hadn't been enough – was it ever? – to watch his own step. He should have taken note where *she* was going. There were no half measures this time, she had started to shake. Was there anything worse than a woman, or a man, who shook?

'You're cold,' he said. 'Let me get a blanket.'

Let him nothing: she had his hand in both hers and was snuffling into his palm, kissing, he had to suppose. Or it was deprivation, a hunger of the senses for taste and smell and touch.

He could feel himself warming to the idea of a sex-starved woman, though he still felt a proper reluctance to get into an animal lather over Carrie Nussbaum. Not because he disliked or despised her; she neither attracted nor repelled him. It was simply the sum of his reservations. She was not for mauling.

Obviously she didn't feel the same. Those badly-hung thighs of hers had been predisposed, more than ready, from the moment she walked into his room. They were quivering beside him now. Someone said it was bad form for a man to refuse to make love to a woman who desired him.

'Look –' look at the fireworks, look at the stars, but don't look at me, I've got a headache – 'there'll be dancing in the Place. It has to be seen, it's something out of Breughel.' A series of pawnbrokers' balls, red, green and yellow, appeared in the sky. By their light he observed that her knees looked medieval too, big and knobbly, like a martyr's.

Next moment a rocket sheared the air and exploded in a shower of sparks. She turned to him with a violence he would not have believed her capable of. Pressed against him, she openly and shamelessly begged.

He thought Good Christ, this is too much. The erotic and the holy joining up in his bed was bad enough: with concentration he might adjust to it, might even enjoy it. But jazzed up with the spirit of carnival –

132

'We're going to be sorry,' he said.

Twoomey's hat bothered Bysshe. There had been funny hats before at Ile-Marie: Bysshe himself had sported a bowls' panama with a pimple in the crown and had passed it on to Gluvas. The bushwhacker was incongruous here as it had not been in Africa where everything was ingested.

With his jeans tucked into canvas boots, the hat set back on his ears, Twoomey was a cowpunch strayed on to the wrong set. He was in exultant mood, aiming a heathen kick at the Christ's Thorn as he passed. 'I've got pictures worth a million words.'

'Not a million of mine,' said Hilda.

'I have to thank you,' Twoomey was addressing Bysshe. 'If I hadn't come here I wouldn't have seen the most telling thing I or anyone else ever captured on film.'

Hilda said, 'We get the feeling that this is where we keep coming in.'

'I can create a Dutch still life with a can of beans and a meat loaf. Or I can make those beans fat and sweet and vulgar, so your mouth waters for them. I can do a mail-order shot of plastic bowls so they look like Ming china. That's advertising.'

'What's this about?' said Bysshe.

'Can't you guess?' said Hilda.

'Here's something I don't have to sell. The statement's made, and it's plain enough for a child to understand.'

'What statement?'

'The more you look, the more you see. It goes way back.' Twoomey couldn't keep still, he was doing restricted gallops to and fro. 'This is Bible stuff!'

'What is?'

'If it was man and monkey it would be evolution.' He fired a forefinger into the air. 'But it's man and devil. Each one of us is born with our quota of good and bad. Nobody's pure. We may be any ratio – sixty-forty, twenty-eighty – it doesn't show. But that – what d'you

133

call him? Warboy? – is fifty-fifty and staked out for everyone to see.'

'I asked you not to photograph him.'

'I'm showing him to the world.'

'I forbid it.'

'You can't keep something like that hidden.'

'Something like what? What do you think he is – a monster?'

'You said it, not me. I say he's a prototype of us all and if he doesn't mind being photographed, why should you?'

'He doesn't understand what's going on, and certainly not what it entails.'

Twoomey hung his thumbs in his braces. 'What's it entail?'

Hilda said, 'Are the pictures good?'

'They're terrific. I can talk to him, he did what I said to do: look here, look there, snarl please. It's best when he smiles, because then it's worse. Did you know the human face has an average of eighty muscles? Warboy's is minus half, including the risorial, the one that works the mouth. I turned my hat upside down and fooled about to make him laugh and it was like a horror movie. I got every bit of that boy's war.'

'Would it make a popular science story?'

Bysshe said sharply, 'There is no story.'

Hilda ran a fingernail against her empty glass. 'How's this: he comes from a remote mountain village where they see the sun a couple of days a year, but generally it's fog and ice, so tourists don't visit. The folk are invert and sequestered. The young leave, the oldies stay on, doing what they've always done. They may get washing machines and television, but they retain their old customs. One of which has always been to make a scapegoat carry their sins away. So they can start again with nice clean souls. Is there any drink?' Bysshe brought another bottle. Hilda splashed herself a glassfull. 'If there's anything worse than white wine, it's red.'

'I read that story,' said Twoomey. 'They draw lots and whoever gets the short straw is stoned to death.'

134

Bysshe realized that anger would put him at a disadvantage. These two would play patball with him. 'That's superstition, not science.'

'It's basic shrink,' Hilda said. 'And popular. What does he do for sex?'

'I haven't the slightest idea.'

'That's where it all starts. I'll think of something.' Hilda grimaced at the wine. 'So he's picked – a virgin child – to absolve the sins of his elders. They set fire to him and chase him away. After that his mind goes blank. Naturally.'

'And he's never spoken since. It figures,' said Twoomey.

'He's all locked up. There's dynamite inside him. One day he'll break out and make mayhem. Have you thought about that?'

Twoomey told Bysshe, 'You'd be responsible.'

'He ought to be restrained. Does anyone know he's here?'

'We could go and get shots of the mountains where he comes from.'

'For God's sake! There are no savage or inaccessible ranges –'

Hilda grinned. 'The range is immaterial.'

'Wait till you see what I've been doing. I'll go fetch it.'

As they watched Twoomey gallop away, Hilda said, 'When I first met Nat he was into the Harvey syndrome, doing pictures of people with rabbit shadows.'

'What must I do to convince you that I won't let that boy be pilloried?'

'You're dramatizing again. Nothing's new, not even a bifacial. There'll be some morbid speculation, perhaps some high-tech interest. But it will be shortlived, and the kid won't be quick enough to catch it.'

'He's made his life here. I don't know why, or where he goes when he goes. One day he won't come back. That will be his choice, he does as he likes.'

'What does he like?'

'Living, breathing, putting flowers in his hair, dancing with the geese.'

'He's blocked. Someone should take him in hand,

135

'show him how to face up to himself.'

'And why he shouldn't be happy. He'd learn that soon enough.'

'Why didn't you answer her letters?' Bysshe had been expecting it. Hilda had repossessed Carrie – for the family, for her own purpose – whatever that was. Carrie now would never come to his mind without Hilda coming too. 'She wrote you and her letters were returned to sender.'

'We'd agreed not to write.'

'When she telephoned, you hung up.'

'We had nothing to say.'

'She had. She said it to me.' Hilda's well-fleshed but illiberal lip curled. 'She said she was in love.'

Bysshe had the use of his damaged smile again, until so recently wasted under Zwemmer's whiskers. 'Let's be sensible. I'm pushing fifty and Carrie was – mature.'

'You telling me the menopause isn't real? She was crazy, point. She was crazy about you, and there's where the full point goes.'

'She didn't kill herself on my account.'

'You don't give a monkey's.'

'I've said I'm sorry. We had no future together and we both knew it.'

'She never had a future with anyone. She was a sad sack.' Hilda probably described her eyes as hazel. Certainly they were hard as nuts. 'I guess you didn't find her empty.'

'You're not going to write about us?'

'Would it bother you? It's good publicity. In the grey fact of American life, sex is the bright spot. Twinned with death it's the definitive statement we're all looking for.'

'Do you remember asking if I wondered what sort of business I'm in?'

'This stuff gives me a headache.' Hilda shoved the wine bottle, it teetered on the edge of the table and Bysshe caught it as it fell. 'We were talking about ulcers and I guess they're real if you have them. But my business is with words and there's more than one way of telling the truth.'

'You must know them all.'

'I couldn't use your way.' Bysshe saw the minefield quite clearly. It had been laid by Carrie in all ignorance. A trained sapper could not have done a better job. He felt that Hilda knew his thoughts. She was smiling, warmed to him, as to her victim. 'Your conventional screen-lover is squashed pie. Erckmann wants something different and that's where Warboy can contribute.'

'Leave him out of it.'

'I can't afford to. He's a gift.'

'To your morbid imagination!'

'My professional faculty. You see, you don't inspire me and he does.'

'He's nothing to do with me. He's a stray who happens to have strayed here –'

'You said he was yours. I make that a love story. It will go like this: ageing amorosos – you said that too – parted by a nubile retard with half a face. Mad with jealousy, the lady amoroso junks herself, leaving the man and the boy to consummate their love in a grotto. How does that grip you?'

'I'll sue anyone who prints it.'

'Surviving ageing amoroso finds that ripeness is not all. The question arises, how long can he hold his pubescent lover?'

Even as ribbing it was poor stuff. But hard-nosed. Hilda would leave out as much as she put in, and like self-service, it would be there for people to help themselves.

'It would be naive to ask what happened to scruples.'

'I'll touch on them. Within the framework of the human dilemma.'

'I meant yours. As a matter of interest, what would you write if you didn't dislike me?'

'Honey, I don't dislike you.' She could switch on a beam like a wall-heater. 'You'd have to get to me for that. Like you got to Carrie, but with her it was you *and* the rest. Her husband had left her, she was full of goofballs and you were nobody to love her.'

He had wondered, though not pressingly, what

Carrie was getting from life. He had spared thought to her prospects as he might to those of a caged budgerigar: they were as limited and as inconceivable, and certainly incapable of being implemented by him.

'It didn't make her special, but I guess she thought it did, and she thought you not being able to love her made her very special.' Hilda raised her brows in enlightenment. 'Actually she was just one of the crowd.'

Bysshe preferred to think Hilda wasn't serious. Consistent, she was dangerous: inconsistent, she would be unbeatable.

Twoomey came out of the house firing his finger. 'Tell that boy if he should break his neck he'll have nowhere to put his face.'

'What have you been doing to him?'

'A kindness.'

'What kindness?'

'I showed him his picture.'

'You call it kind to show him a photograph of himself?'

'Not the ones like he is, but one like he ought to be.'

'Invisible,' said Hilda.

'He wanted that picture, he wanted to take it with him. I said you can't have this, it's my only copy. I'll do you another. He was over the moon, he ran out and jumped the stairs. The whole flight. He hit the ground running.'

'Let's see the picture,' said Hilda.

Twoomey had it in the breast pocket of his jacket. He took it out, flourished it and held it up, panning it closely from Hilda to Bysshe. It was a monochrome, head and shoulders of a virtual stranger. Bysshe could detect a teasing resemblance to someone often seen but not known. It made him realize how little he relied on the good half of the oieboy's face. It had always been so composed, untouched by emotion, blush and sweat. The photograph gave the impression of a stone face, a funerary angel's, without a granule of personality and just enough life to open the eyes but not to blink them.

'Classy,' said Hilda.

'It's all wrong.'

138

Twoomey bridled. 'How can it be wrong when it's all right?'

'It's not him.'

'That's because you've never seen him. The two halves of any one face don't match exactly. The pigments and pimples and planes, eyes and ear placements are different on one side than the other. In a normal face they harmonize.'

'How did you get this picture?'

Hilda sighed. 'You really want to know?'

Twoomey hung up his thumbs. 'I took Warboy en face, in full sun, though I didn't get both sides as evenly lit as I'd like. I processed the film, then printed the good side with the other side covered. Reversed the negative, and using a red filter on the enlarger arranged the negative to fit the other half, removed the red filter, printed the other half – holding back the side already exposed and then developed the complete print. Now he's got two good sides and no gothic.'

'It's the completeness that makes it completely wrong.'

'I've given him back his face.'

'Didn't you stop to think what harm that might do?'

'Harm?'

'Showing him what he can never be.'

'Giving him ideas,' said Hilda.

'He's an unknown quantity, totally unpredictable. I never know what he's thinking or what he will do when he's upset.'

'Hell, it's only a gimmick.'

'To you. But to him –'

'He wouldn't know himself,' said Hilda.

'He knew, and he loved it.'

Hilda turned to Bysshe. 'Take us to Nice?'

'When?'

'Now.' She took out a lipstick and drew herself lips in tiger orange.

'I can't, not right away. I've got a flat battery.'

'With a puss like his you don't know if he's mad or glad. But a baby tries to eat something it likes, and he tried to eat that picture.'

139

'Call us a cab.'

'Why do you want to go to Nice?'

'We're leaving.'

Bysshe's heart bounded. He did not have to question it, Twoomey did that.

'Leaving? What about my pictures?'

'We've got all the pictures we need.'

Twoomey aimed his thumb at Bysshe. 'Mug shots of him. I'd like more character.'

'So would I.'

Twoomey grimaced, Hilda went on drawing herself a new mouth, sight unseen.

'What about a flight? You're not booked,' said Bysshe.

'You can get a flight if you pay. Erckmann's paying.'

'He's paying for a story.'

'He'll get it.'

'We haven't discussed it.'

'I never discuss what I write.'

Bysshe could believe it. The wonder was not that she got away with murder, but how she made murder acceptable, enviable. Charismatic. Some people would say he was lucky and that Erckmann had done him a favour by getting Hilda to write about him. But according to Twoomey she had badgered Erckmann for the assignment. Why? She must know that her stories were considered an underwrite. If Hilda Latouche did a piece about you it was a guarantee you would be talked of whatever the world news, and remembered wherever a morbid few were gathered together. It posed the question: if publicity was amoral, but like daylight you had to have it, why should Hilda be doing him a favour? The answer was that she wouldn't. She wasn't.

The matter of Carrie Nussbaum who might, or might not, be related to Hilda by marriage; who might, or might not, be dead by her own hand, was incidental. He couldn't help thinking how like Carrie it was to be immaterial. Absurd to think she could kill herself because of him, and absurdity, too, was beside the point. So was the question of what Hilda chose to believe. The fact somewhere at issue was that Hilda had it in for him.

'Erckmann will be happy,' she said.

'I'd like to be happy too.'

She parted her new lips in a lovely smile. She could, on occasion, look enchanting: one had to remember that sorcery was a big pond. 'Are you worried about something?'

'I don't care what you do about me –'

'That's sensible. Your public image is at the stage where it can only be done good to. The problem has been what to do. I never do snow jobs.'

'So far as Carrie's concerned, I have nothing to be ashamed of. Or regret. We were comfortable together, she stayed as long as it suited her and left to rejoin her party when they went home. We both knew that was as far as it went. We were being our age.'

'Hers was a climacteric. If that doesn't worry you, what does?'

'The thought that you're planning to use the boy, make him into a freak show.'

'How would I do that?'

'Simply by writing about him. Making people aware of his existence.'

'He's at least as remarkable as the white rhino. A lot of people will want to remark on him.'

'Conservationists?' suggested Twoomey.

'Psychophysicists, psychobiologists, physiognomists. Anyone who thinks your fate is in your face is going to be interested in his split level.'

'He ought to be seen,' said Twoomey. 'There were faces back from Vietnam getting fixed as good as new. Someone might do as much for him.'

'Is that a nice thought?' said Bysshe.

'It may surprise you to know –' Twoomey aimed between Bysshe's eyes – 'we communicate, Warboy and me. We understand each other. Empathy is what you need in visual art. You learn to get into the skin of the girl or the brick – whatever it is you're photographing. I'll show you three sides of the brick and one of the nude, but I'll show some of her inside as well.'

'How do you get into the skin of a brick?'

'Mind you –' Twoomey was set to roller on – 'it takes

more than practice to get the feel of people –'

'Call the cab and collect your gear, Nat.'

'I promised the kid his picture.'

'There's an afternoon flight we can make.'

Twoomey might fire his fingers, Hilda held the lipstick like a bullet in hers. Muttering, Twoomey went away.

'Must you go?' Bysshe could still arrange his features to look wistful, though he was now aware that crowsfeet and puckering round the mouth lent him a certain wryness.

Nut-eyed, Hilda showed her kernels. 'You've never had a genuine emotion for anyone. That's not a crime, but we were talking about love, and I question how many people know what it is.'

'Do you?'

'Thank Christ I don't make my living pretending I do. You'd like to be that old sweet Zwemmer, all loving and giving. And you looked the part till I made you shave him off.'

So of his hating man, the leper doctor who hated lepers, not a glimpse had come through. Hilda was more than usually perceptive and if she saw no hidden depth in his performance, the average audience certainly wouldn't. He had too well concealed the misanthrope under the beard.

It gave him a jolt before he reflected that Hilda's function – and privilege – was to cut the ground from under his feet. Anyway, his purpose had been served. He had used a ploy to deceive the camera.

What mattered was the result, getting a good one, *any* good one. He had got what would be seen as a simple turncoat case, black turning white, the sinner turning martyr. No rage, no deviousness. It happened all the time, all historical time, anyway, and to the average audience it would be acceptable. Wheels within wheels had no place on the big screen. He had better be satisfied. It was a compliment to be accused by Hilda, especially by Hilda, of living the part. The irony he could reserve to himself.

'Never mind,' she said, 'you're a hairy man, you'll soon grow him back.'

They heard Twoomey come bursting out of the house, effecting an explosion between the door jamb and himself. He shouldered through the rosemary, achieving a burst of sweetness, and stood before them, his breath gathered like a child's ready to scream.

There was nothing childish about his veins, a zigzag red and purple bunch pulsated on his temple.

'Did you call the cab?'

Twoomey's hands seemed to be sticky. He scrubbed them on his chest, leaving stains which were almost certainly blood.

'Have you been messing with fixers?'

'I think he's cut himself,' said Bysshe.

Twoomey fired a bloody finger. 'I hold you responsible!'

'Sorry. I keep meaning to cut back the thorn hedge.'

'For damage to my property while on your premises!'

'Damage? Property?'

'I had the best part of my stuff in your bathroom - lenses, film, filter, fuses, adaptors - my tripod's turned inside out, my changing-bag's ripped up, my enlarger's been stomped on -'

'You don't say,' said Hilda.

'But who would do it?'

'I'm giving you one guess!'

There was a pause. Bysshe said 'Look -' without knowing what he wanted looked at.

Twoomey shouted, '*You* look! He goes to the darkroom and junks everything. It so happens I keep my cameras under my bed or I'd have lost them too -'

'Why would he do that?'

'He's crazy, he's hyped, he's certifiable!'

'He's harmless.'

'How do you know? You said yourself you don't know what he'll do.'

'There would have to be a reason.'

'Maybe he didn't like his picture after all.' Hilda yawned. 'It could be he thinks if you've got his likeness you've got his mana.'

Twoomey exhaled, 'Lord Christ, I'm going to get *him*!' and shot away under his own steam. The rosemary rocked, again there was a burst of sweetness which gave

Bysshe, at this inopportune moment, a pang of pure nostalgia.

'I wonder did he call the cab?' said Hilda.

'Will he do anything violent?'

'I shouldn't think so. His violence is confined to his blood vessels.' Bysshe got to his feet. Hilda said, 'Check on the taxi.'

Bysshe ran down to the orchard. If it was only a question of running, the boy could outdistance Twoomey. But if Twoomey took him unawares – of course he couldn't do that while the geese were about.

But the geese were resting under the trees, a flotilla of white one-masters. They heard Bysshe approaching. They stretched their necks and began the slow gargle which preceded full-throat alarm. Bysshe turned back.

As always, a passage in that dry land was susurration. He paused occasionally to listen. The geese had subsided, the cicadas were part of the vegetation, the barking of a dog far away in the valley enhanced the silence. To Bysshe the silence sounded ominous. He would have called out, but was prevented by indecision about what to call. He had not been on Christian name terms with Twoomey and to shout his surname would be peremptory and might enrage him further.

He took a short cut and was winded climbing the scarp. Twoomey stood at the entrance to the grotto. There was a stillness about him, an arrest. He was watching but he wasn't poised, he wasn't even waiting. Bysshe stopped to draw breath and Twoomey acknowledged his presence by blowing a sharp blast through closed lips.

The boy was inside the grotto with his back to them, facing the mirror propped on the rock ledge. He was positioning and re-positioning Twoomey's hat. He set it squarely over his brows, snatched it off, furled it, punched the crown and lodged it on his ears.

Then he removed it, and holding it in both hands lowered it slowly on to his head. Bysshe was reminded of the scene in *Richard the Third* when Olivier tried on the crown. The boy adjusted the hat, tilting and tipping it ever lower. When he turned to face them, the brim was pulled down over his right side and raked high over the left. His calcined cheek twitched in the spasm which served him for a smile.

Twoomey spoke with awe. 'You know something? He's conceited.'

4

I used to think there was a reason for me being as I am, and all I had to do was dig the reason up. I thought we were a single unit, separated for living purposes. I thought that for years. Doug never did. I suppose it was a kink left over from the womb and I was the one who got it.

People talked about us when we were in our pram. They talked above us as if we were animals that couldn't understand. But a baby knows if it's being passed over. I knew, and I let them know I knew. They said, 'She's got a paddy on her, if nothing else.' And Doug would look up with his sweet hurt look – hurt, mind you, though he'd been dealt all the aces. That look is one of the aces.

When we were out of infant school they cut off his curls. I screamed and screamed, trying to make them understand that we were really one person and it was my hair they had cut off. They put me in the meter-cupboard to calm down.

Later on, when I knew about how babies were made, I blamed my mother. She should never have had twins if she couldn't divide us properly.

I haven't been clever and I haven't been lucky. Luck isn't something you're entitled to, and the way things have turned out there's not much to choose between us. Doug's had what I wanted, but he couldn't take it. I could have taken it, but didn't get it. Our plusses and minusses are mixed up.

*

He sent tickets for the première of his new film. Pike said he wasn't going: 'If I saw him I'd knock him down.' He blames Doug for everything.

But we watched the ballyhoo on television. It was wet on the night of the première, and rain either makes things look more expensive than they are, or very, very cheap. The cars arriving at the West End cinema sparkled like diamonds. Even the gutters twinkled. In the foyer the diamonds were smaller and had to contend with platinum blondes and blazing shirt fronts. There was a superior moral tone – a big donation was being made to leprosy research – and Royals were present. We had a back view of Doug bowing over their hands. He has poise. Even when he was at the pimply stage he could charm the pretty girls into getting up to dance with him.

'This sort of thing makes me sick,' said Pike.

It would. But there are so many sicknesses: fear, envy, hunger, rage, disgust, and simple stomachache. And longing: I know about that.

'It's his living,' I said.

Pike doesn't understand finesse. He showed me what he thinks it is, waggled his bottom, smirked and fluttered two fingers in the air. Then switched off the television.

I made him come with me to see the film when it was generally released. He said he didn't want to watch Doug poncing about and I said that was what I wanted. I wanted to see him making his living.

There isn't any poncing in this film. Doug takes the part of a doctor who went to Africa to look after lepers. I hardly recognized him. He was made up with a bushy wig, beard and false eyebrows. He stooped from his shoulders so that his neck stuck out like a tortoise's: he dragged one leg and whipped the other along with a stick. They had emphasized every line on his face and added more. Only his eyes were the same. Only Doug looks at you like that.

Pike sat beside me, giving the screen all his attention, his bones creaking now and then – they do if he's still for more than two minutes at a time. Then they started showing close-ups of sores crawling with maggots,

148

stumps of limbs, children covered with flies. And a face like a rotten apple, eaten to the core.

Pike jumped up and pushed his way out, not giving me or anyone else time to move aside. A woman at the end of the row with a shopping bag in her lap had the contents tipped out into the aisle.

I followed him, stepping over margarine, cracked eggs, crinkle chips and a spilt kilo bag of sugar. We left a first-hand drama going on which must have entertained some people more than the one on the screen.

Pike made straight for the car. He got in and sat behind the wheel, making no attempt to open the passenger door for me. I had to bang on the window to remind him to release the lock.

I said, 'You know you started a cake-mix without a mixing bowl back there?'

He put his hand over his face. 'I can see it now.'

'Let's go before they get our number.'

'I shall never forget it.'

'The memory will fade.'

'It brought it all back.'

'Don't fret, they'll clean the carpet,' I said. 'It must have to take a lot of rough treatment.'

'It finished us – Cherrimay and me.'

To do myself justice, I knew what had started and where it was going. I just didn't want to go with it. Some things shouldn't be remembered in company. Any company is wrong, and Pike's is lethal.

'That face –'

'If you won't drive, I will.' I leaned across and switched on the engine.

'It was because of him she had the abortion. She was afraid she'd have a baby with a face like his.'

'If Cherrimay had an abortion it was because she didn't want to have a baby – any baby.'

'What do you mean "if"? She killed our child because of what she saw at your brother's.'

We'd been through this before, none of it was new. I'd seen Pike weep, he sheds tears like other men sweat. Any delicate sensitivity is liable to get swamped.

Personally I don't believe there was an abortion. I

149

don't believe Cherrimay Pugh was pregnant, and certainly not by Pike. The whole thing was so convenient – an anticlimax. One day we had the lover-child, carrying within her the future of the race – Pike's race – the guarantee of man- and woman-hood both: the next we had a burnt soul, she'd been through the fire, she was all dignity acquired by suffering. Sinned against.

I wasn't present at the monumental row there must have been. Darlene was. 'He stamped up and down, shouting, I thought he'd have gone through the floor. He was like a man possessed. You know what I mean?'

'I know.'

'He kept shouting "Why? Why?"' – which was taking the word out of Darlene's mouth – but she had countered with, 'What else could we do?'

'Did he tell you?'

'He called us murderers and kicked my sideboard. You want to be careful of him, he's unbalanced, he could do you an injury.'

'I know.'

I daresay Darlene will leak more information in due time. But I've already made up my mind. I don't believe Darlene could organize an abortion, she wouldn't know where to begin. Cherrimay just might. But then she's capable – she's most capable – of organizing the whole nothing.

Pike is a believer, he has to be. I don't grudge him his faith.

'You know what I think?' He knows I know, he has told me often enough. He is going to tell me again. 'Your brother's a pervert. He gets a kick out of this sort of thing.'

'What sort of thing?'

'He didn't have to act the part, he really loved messing with those lepers.' I had seen that he hated it. Doug has to be different from his natural self and it comes over big on the big screen. 'You know what I think – I think that sort of thing turns him on. That's why he keeps the boy.'

'The boy's gone. No one knows where. And Doug's living in Greece.'

Does it matter what Pike thinks? Only to Pike. And his memory is short, he is a survivor.

But I can't help being conscious of what he thinks, even when he isn't thinking it. His thoughts coexist with my moment of glory.

'A kid with half a face!'

But a whole man. Pike doesn't know what I'm thinking.

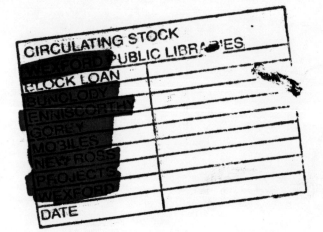